The Total View *of* Taftly

The Total View *of* Taftly

A NOVEL

scott morris

d

HILL STREET PRESS
Athens, Georgia

A HILL STREET PRESS BOOK

Published in the United States of America by
Hill Street Press LLC   191 East Broad Street, Suite 209
Athens, Georgia 30601-2848 USA   706-613-7200
info@hillstreetpress.com   www.hillstreetpress.com

Hill Street Press is committed to preserving the written word. Every effort is made to print books on acid-free paper with a significant amount of post-consumer recycled content.   ~ This is a work of fiction. All names, characters, places, and situations are either products of the author's imagination or are used fictitiously. No reference to any real person, living or deceased, is intended nor should be inferred, and any similarity is entirely coincidental.   ~ No material in this book may be reproduced, scanned, stored, or transmitted in any form, including all electronic and print media, or otherwise used without the prior written consent of the publisher. However, an excerpt not to exceed 500 words may be used one time only by newspaper and magazine editors solely in conjunction with a review of or feature article about this book, the author, or Hill Street Press, LLC. Attribution must be provided including the publisher's name, author's name, and title of the book.

Library of Congress Cataloging-in-Publication Data

Morris, Scott M., 1966–
    The total view of Taftly / by Scott Morris.
        p.   cm.
    ISBN 1-892514-70-2 (alk. paper)
    1. Young men–Mississippi–Fiction. 2. Philosophers–Fiction. 3. Mississippi–Fiction.
4. Weight loss–Fiction. I. Title.

    PS3563.O2439 T68 2000
    813'.54–dc21

                                                    99-089072

ISBN # 1-892514-70-2
10   9   8   7   6   5   4   3   2   1
First printing

Dedication

TK

Acknowledgements

TK

PART
1

Taftly Harper had been away for awhile. When he returned, it took the regulars by surprise. This was a whole new Taftly.

In the back of the bar, floating atop a turbulent turquoise sea of decaying enamel, hung a photograph of Taftly's granddaddy, whiskered and fierce. The granddaddy had been lean and capable, and Taftly's appearance made a few of the men remark upon the far reach of his genes, finally pushing aside the fatty ones Taftly had inherited from his mother.

Taftly told everyone his obesity had simply become boring. Having arrived at a sluggish sobriety upon his twentieth white Russian some three months ago, he'd hobbled down to the corner store where he noticed a running magazine. A half-naked female runner smiled at him from the cover. Her brown skin smiled at Taftly, too, and Taftly began to smile back, envisioning a merry chase and seduction, shiny, healthy thighs about his person, and he, Taftly, venturing into a realm of love only available to the beautiful people. His entire life Taftly had wanted to love and be loved in return, and to nurture his romance with at least occasional visitations of bravery and splendor. Yet here he was, not far from thirty, with only one relationship under his belt, tending toward failure and stunning mediocrity.

The sight of his own body later that evening terrified him into discipline. It brought to mind a bloated terrapin stripped of its shell and gone ripe in the noon sun. He wept for himself, gathered his aggrieved member and howled apologies for leaving it stranded amidst so much extraneous mass.

Early the next morning, Taftly managed a mile. It was to be the first of five, but his confrontation with gravity proved so debilitating he was left gasping alongside a ditch. He felt as if he were wearing a sweat suit packed with stewed lard. He yearned to run fast enough to actually slough off about forty excess pounds at once, ridding himself of blubber by achieving Gs, such as fighter pilots do when breaking the sound barrier. But after fifty yards, Taftly saw he was hardly moving at all. His momentum was principally a coordinated falling forward. He did this heavily. And there were other problems.

"They never mentioned penis placement in the magazines," he huffed. He imagined half the battle of running to be the degrading business of keeping his tallywacker from getting plastered full up against his stomach. Still, he kept at it, taking in mile after mile, day-in, day-out, until, months later, he was lean and far along toward a tan.

Returning to the bar, he anticipated instant romance and of

a very high quality. Throughout the half-mile walk into town he had been imagining a girl as fit and glittery as himself, though he hoped she would have come by it naturally. Like all hard earners, he envied those who were simply born with the best qualities.

As he sipped a preliminary beer—the better to savor the bourbon which would arrive as an awaited entree—he surmised he would court the girl slowly, showing her a gentleman's turns. There would be two dates, exotic yet tasteful, then a picnic, and finally a run to bind her to him. Taftly's striding posture, Taftly felt, was exceptionally upright and determined. Going into the second mile, he believed his gait to be greatly sexual. Once she'd witnessed his second-mile stride, she would be flummoxed with desire for him, for Taftly.

His bar friends could believe it. They were simply astonished at the new Taftly, though one, a pathetic minion named Oswald, insisted that while Taftly was thinner, he seemed to have advanced well up in years.

"You may have that rare disease," Oswald announced. He appeared genuinely concerned and backed away as if confronting something bubonic. "You know them children with big heads and wrinkles and gray hair? They reach a hundred years in two decades and die of old age before their high school proms."

The others, however, kept telling Taftly what a marvel his new self was. Taftly smiled and raised his glass to each compliment. "It would be good if she could walk in while such kind things are being said about me," he whispered. But an hour passed and no one fitting the description of Taftly's dream girl entered the bar. The thought occurred to him that a girl like the girl he'd seen on the cover of the running magazine might lack passion. That woman had been wrong all along. "Taftly," Taftly said. "You can't even conceive of her."

His heart felt pure then, and he saw himself as a very fancy golden retriever with a good pedigree, waiting on a bone from his master. This, Taftly reckoned, was the Total View, and he should always keep it in mind.

Because he'd run better than ten miles that day, Taftly splurged and ordered a double bourbon on the rocks. His first sip would have been glorious had it not been for Oswald, who had spotted some commotion outside the bar.

"That there is what you call two Buicks fightin' fer the same parking space," Oswald cried out, slapping Taftly's back.

It was the Clydesdale twins. They were big, ankleless, and glutted with superfluous neck and teat. This did nothing to discourage them from mini-skirts, hot-pants and tube-tops, however.

Taftly's throat clinched stiff as a gourd when he saw them. After months of readying himself—on one long run he'd hit "the wall" and imagined he'd passed beyond thin directly into a girlish nubile—he was having to deal with Oswald and the Clydesdales, Trixie and Trina. It hardly seemed fair. It was something from his old fat loser's life.

"They act like they might be on fire. Move right quick for girls their size," Oswald noted.

The Clydesdale's T-top Camaro had been abandoned in the middle of the street, and the twins were jumping around with a kind of energy Taftly considered inappropriate to persons of their girth. Furthermore, Trixie had a stark mad look which reminded him of the sex act. He knew immediately it was how he had appeared years ago when he'd been taken by Ruby Cally, his first serious girlfriend.

This hurt Taftly's feelings. Being svelte had made him tender, even more tender than the former Taftly who was known for being a bit of a cry baby. Ruby had made a game of hurting his feelings. "You hurt my feelings," Taftly would say. "Your feelings suck," Ruby would tell him. And so on.

They had had sex only once. Ruby feared it would at some point lead to suffocation. Taftly's arms weren't strong enough to keep him safely aloft in her opinion. After that, Taftly developed the theory that for a person of his enormity—stature is the word he used—sex was undesirable. There had been many hefty holy men down through the ages, and Taftly saw every chance of success in joining their number. He grew sideburns and perused the Scriptures for obese Biblical heroes, astounded that so many of the Hebrews were handsome and strongly desirous of carnal knowledge. Less than a week after his monkish vow, he began to wonder how long he could remain celibate and youthful. Crook in hand, his mind wandered from shepherd girl to shepherd girl and eventually lingered along sweet brooks and lush valleys, where Taftly always inhaled deeply of the roses.

To make up for the death of his father—actually his father had simply left town one day but Taftly preferred to think of him as deceased—Taftly's mother had always taken a tireless interest in Taftly. On Saturday evenings, when Taftly might have been out with his peers, he and his mother would clutch each other's elbows and enact big persons' versions of dances to Glenn Miller recordings. Sometimes Taftly combed her hair.

Not without reason, she claimed to be able to read his mind. After Taftly's despicable session with Ruby, for instance, his mother detected the remains of their transgression as soon as Taftly walked through the door. It startled her out of her wits. "Taftly! Taftly! Taftly!" she bawled, then broke down completely. Taftly wanted to comfort her, but the scent of Ruby wafted from his flanks and he ran to the bathroom.

Three days after Taftly graduated from high school, his mother died. Though the entire town showed up for the funeral, Taftly perceived there was something second-rate about the proceedings and concluded that he and his mother had not existed at all.

His granddaddy, by contrast had departed in grand style. Before being buried, his grumpy corpse was driven round the town square three times to quench the thirst of mourners. He'd founded a bank, fought in the First World War and given the local college—which Taftly's great-granddaddy, a Confederate veteran, had started—enough money to add to their library and build several new dormitories. The town and the college named a day after him, and when he persisted in getting the ban on alcohol repealed, the first bar in town—the bar Taftly frequented—had been named the Copiah Harper Tavern in his honor. As far as anyone knew, Taftly's granddaddy had only done one thing wrong in his life—he'd reared a gadabout son, the feckless Julius Harper. Taftly won much affection from the elders simply by despising his own father.

As Taftly struggled with the other pallbearers to get his mother safely under the funeral tent, he thought of his father. Everywhere he looked, his father was not there, just as he expected. He did, however, notice a group of college boys tipping a fifth of bourbon and lollygagging amongst the tombstones. Taftly believed it was the most impertinent thing he'd ever witnessed and would have gone to see about them with his fists had it not been for the business at hand. In a perfect world, cemeteries and colleges would be separated by long, difficult miles, he mused.

Though the interlopers eventually wandered from sight, Taftly grew more agitated. The rather good sermon preached by Pastor Bates was lost on him completely, and after the service he refused to leave the grave site. Taftly was uninterested in returning to an empty house, Taftly said. He wanted to remain with what was left of his family.

Later that afternoon, three men arrived wearing grey work slacks and pitted undershirts. They carried shovels and went quietly about their work. Taftly watched their progress, convinced he should do something about it. If he would not beg God to resurrect his mother, he could at least reach out his hands to stop the steady shower of dirt slowly covering her, but he did nothing and the burial was at last completed. When the cemetery seemed properly deserted, Taftly lay across the front row of folding chairs and cried.

Several hours later he woke from a thick slumber to discover the college boys had him surrounded. They wore vests and three-button suits, attire you would not expect from a backwoods college. The tall one with red hair possessed a merchaum pipe. "That's freshly dug," he said, nodding. Taftly could scarcely credit the kindness in the young man's voice. He found himself warming to it, reaching for the proffered hand.

"My mother," Taftly said.

"We're sorry for your grief," the red-head told him.

Taftly drank with them by his mother's grave. The college boys comforted him, telling him of a coterie they'd founded for the express purpose of exploring literature and feeling exquisite passion. Many on campus believed they were queer, they explained. "But the fact is, we're—each of us—awaiting a whole other category of woman. Our women will not come from these parts or any parts like these parts," one of the group declared. Taftly agreed. He believed his woman would be found with their women.

That fall he enrolled in the college. He took to books heedlessly, reading with something approaching anger and believing everything he read. By his sophomore year, he'd come under the spell of so many philosophies and writers he puked up learning like a juke box gone haywire. Aristotle, Marx,

Tolstoy, Flaubert—he was for all of them. Presently, he discovered he'd far out-read the others in the coterie, and Collins, the red-headed leader, soured on him because of this. When he caught Taftly with *Time Regained,* it proved to be the final straw. The audacity of actually reading all of Proust could not be tolerated. Plus, Taftly looked incredibly shabby in a vest and three-button suit and was a cause of sniggering for petite co-eds.

When Collins evicted Taftly—telling him to never wear corduroy if he knew what was good for a man of his bulk—Taftly thought of Marx. It seemed impossible suddenly that he had wasted so much time in college, roosting grounds of the petty bourgeoisie and their decadent commitments to fashion, when all along he might have been plowing a field or wrenching something with the working man.

Within the week he was employed by Copiah Springs Bottled Water Company, a holding of his family's, and since Taftly was the lone survivor, a holding of Taftly's. He drove a pretty green truck and delivered jugs of spring water welled from Copiah Springs. The company president urged Taftly to consider a management position, but Taftly's intentions prevailed.

Aside from the Bible, he left off books entirely. Years passed and he became chummy with his old high school friends who had not had the cleverness for college and were pleased to see one of their own brought down to size. He forgot most of what he'd learned and sought happiness in common things like candy corns and Chick-o-sticks. Wallowing about his house, he'd sometimes beller for his mother, gone, indecently it seemed, into the gaping earth, where he often wished to follow.

But then he had come upon the runner's magazine that fine day in June, finding, to his surprise, that his heart had not aged at all and his head remained full of wild dreams and longing.

II

WHAT THE CLYDESDALES WERE UP TO was anyone's guess, but there was no ignoring them. It seemed they were either in terrible pain or afflicted with spontaneous orgasms. Both had narrow eyes deeply set in considerable fat canyons, as if their very faces were competing with the Wild West and all its craggy wonders. Both were pale. Compared to the rest of their bodies, their heads appeared shrunken and deflated. Since their arches had long ago collapsed from the terrible weight above, they were in the habit of wearing cheap flat sneakers or cowboy boots with the heels levelled off specially for them by a destitute country cobbler who sometimes got felt up for his trouble. Atop their heads rested snakey coils of highly coiffed curls, each ringlet severely bleached and crisp. And while they were always maneuvering their tongues in the coquettish manner of their screen idol, Marilyn Monroe, the main impression they gave was of two seriously heavy women about to succumb to epilepsy.

Back in high school, they were merely prissy and terrible to look at. Taftly had been their favorite because they believed he was on their team in the coming world conflict of considerable people versus those who were too negligible to count at all, as in anyone under two hundred pounds. Napoleon was Trixie's idea of a snack cracker and could not be taken seriously as a leader. Henry the VIII, now there was a man of substance. They longed to travel back and offer up themselves on a platter of cold roast beef and mutton. They dreamed of the mead-quaffing Henry slapping them around with enormous drumsticks and smearing grease across their quaking thighs before taking them mid-feast, as if they were simply another course.

But as they got older, they began to somehow believe they weren't larded at all. There was no reason for them to come to this conclusion, yet they did, eventually becoming stylish in a regrettably whorish Helmut Newton sort of way.

When Taftly went out to the street to see what was the matter, he was ambushed by a fuselage of meaty breast. This was Trina. One of her bosoms had disgorged and slapped the too-near Taftly in the kisser. Trina wedged it back. "There's a bed of fire ants in our car somehow," she crooned. Her voice seemed to be a cross between a yodel and the terrified bleating of a goat being electrocuted by way of a cattle prod jacked into its hind portal.

As Taftly and Oswald helped remove the ants, a ghastly variety of hard rock music caterwauled from the stereo of the

Camaro. Taftly recognized the tasteless ditty as Loverboy's "Only The Lucky Ones," which he took to be a bad omen.

The fellows from the bar were chortling and taking bets on something, Taftly would never know what. This was precisely what they liked about their old bar, the comic squalor. Just last week an elderly drunk had become outlandish over a show tune. Attempting to tap dance, he'd broken an ankle. Hoards of piggish faces gathered around shouting encore, thinking his fall was part of the act.

Oswald was searching an ant out from Trixie's gorge when she whacked the Pabst Blue Ribbon right out of his hand. The can danced up against his face but did not adhere, as if Oswald were a failing magnet. When it hit his shoes, he pretended nothing had happened, looking elsewhere as he stooped to retrieve it. "Sure," he said.

Taftly believed the ants had all been found but could not persuade the others. The twins were wearing denim shorts so tight their thighs looked to be exploding out from them. Their inseams were hellishly cloven. The horrendous moaning had not abated, either, and shortly another boob flopped out from its macramé container. This wasn't at all what Taftly had in mind. It bordered on the Satanic, something only his former pal Dante could have thought of.

"You sweet help," one of the Clydesdales was braying.

"Anytime, ladies, anytime," Oswald crowed.

Trixie and Trina would have given more consideration to a toilet seat. They shot Oswald a threatening look and then returned to Taftly. A snippet of tit, like the last sliver of a bad day's sunset, peeked from Trina's tube-top. Most horrible was the fact that Taftly felt a slight flutter below.

"Y'all sassy," Oswald squawked, still believing he mattered.

"We'll sit on you, crush you," Trixie told him. She sent the Pabst flying again and Oswald shuffled back into the bar, already preparing to lie to the others with a story about how the twins had offered him a quicky.

"Lookit-*thar*. Mmm. *Little*," Trina grunted, punching Taftly's arm.

In the future, Taftly would associate the broken cadences of the Clydesdales with the snorting and stomping accomplished by a bull before it mounts up. When they resisted prepositions and proper names, it meant they were of a mind for union. But Taftly hadn't learned that yet, and when the Clydesdales asked him if they might give him a ride home, he thought it would be all right since he was in no condition to encounter his dream girl anymore.

Less than a mile from town they started tasking him with questions about what it must have been like, going from heavy to slight. It fascinated them, their old team-mate almost vanishing like that. They began pawing him a little.

"I live, hey, actually, listen, I live the other way actually," Taftly said.

"Actually, actually! Them's smart words. They said you went through one a them book phases. *Actually*, we gone talk," Trixie told him.

Trina turned off the road and tore across a field as if hounded by the law. Everything the twins did suggested they were being pursued, wanted. It was perhaps their most revolting characteristic.

Suddenly the Camaro cleared a creek bed like something custom-made for television. When the car landed, Trina's boobs flew up around her face, her chin valleying the cleavage. "Oops!" she shrieked. She offered Taftly a cameo wink—a plumped diva for a dark De Mille—then hit the gas and sped along giggling.

Trixie squeezed Taftly's knee as the car slowed to park. "You little bitty," she said. She began spritzing herself with something that sparkled and smelled of spoiled peaches.

"But he used to be—" Trina belched ruthlessly and passed a pint of rum to her sibling. "Big," she concluded.

"Did it happen everwhare?" Trixie questioned. The girls guffawed over that one for awhile, spritzing and chewing gum.

"I really should get home," Taftly said.

He was feeling a crush of anxiety. It pocked him with oily perspiration. His eyes burned. Then they burned the more because Trina began spritzing Taftly's face, sending shots of peachy glitter directly into his irises. There ensued a tustle of sorts after which Taftly looked like something basted up for a perverse beauty pageant.

"Come on, little bitty," Trixie demanded. She jerked him by the collar.

Taftly fought for awhile but it only seemed to entice them. He realized the one way to prevail was to initiate something completely unchivalrous, like kneeing them between the legs, but he couldn't bring himself to do it and so they brought him down. Purblind and paralyzed by disbelief, it did not seem to Taftly that this could be happening. He felt enormously tired.

Trina straddled his chest, and presented her breasts as if they were precious heirlooms, while Trixie went for his privates.

"Rough his engine some," Trina called.

"This lil' thang?" Trixi barked.

"Yeah. Race at li'l bitch 'til it backfires er somethin.'"

When Taftly started to cry, it made them more urgent. His pain was delicious to them.

"You shouldn't have gone small, little bitty," Trina told him, pinching herself for added ecstasy. She was slobbering wildly, sending flecks of hot spittle everywhere.

"Betray us," Trixie whispered heavily. "Yes, betray us. Oh, this what you get."

Realizing Trixie was actually going to try to service herself with him, he began to fight again and beat them back. He did so without dignity, slapping and clawing at their faces like a child until he had gained his feet and stood uncertainly with his pants about his calves. When he reached to pull up his britches, Trina assaulted him with a right cross. He fell backward, and the girls began to cackle and attack him with their feet. Taftly felt as if he were being stampeded by two elephants drugged to their tusks on amphetamines.

Eventually they finished stomping and drove away. Bruised and battered, Taftly watched stars sprout in the sky. When the cool of evening arrived, he restored himself as best he could and began walking home.

It had never occurred to him that a man could be the target of an attempted rape and not like it. During his religious period of swearing off coitus, he'd sometimes imagined roving bands of evil women overtaking him on the way home from school. They did everything, repeatedly. But these rogues were natural blonds somewhere in the neighborhood of 110 pounds. They spoke harshly but could not relent from caressing him and agonizing over the beauty of his manhood. In this way, he was appreciated and made to do everything, not a lick of it his fault, either.

Taftly felt of his behind, though nothing had happened to it. From his neck down he felt rudely soiled, and his head seemed to condemn him from a distance and not be a part of him at all. "I must admit it's not the same as if I were a woman," he said meekly. "But it—"

He began to cry again. He believed that now he had been ruined and would never find his dream of love. A strange leprosy was at work, chiefly attacking his loins. Though he did not quite believe his unit would fall off, already it was becoming odious and useless. This new sickness left the body intact but unworthy, Taftly noticed, and he knew instinctively the doctors could do nothing for it.

For the next few months he read books about rape and identified his every nuerosis. He imagined, for instance, that in his ant picking he'd actually led the Clydesdales to believe he wanted it. And going from fat to thin, from their world to a more subtle one, wasn't that like taunting them, like wearing a skirt hiked up in a dark alley? Perhaps they'd seen him running when he'd "hit the wall," preening along in his new weight. What right did he have to lord exercise over them? Why, he'd drawn them in, had been asking for it all along. A still pearled voice denied all of this, but it did so from far away, as if it could not endure approaching his corrupted frame.

Much of this was expected—he'd found it in the books he'd snuck from the library. He couldn't check them out because a co-ed at the college might be raped at some point, and his library record would reveal him to be a suspect. The Clydesdales had made him paranoid. They'd pulled back the curtains on a darkling world. How strange that he'd once conceived of himself as unhappy. Looking back, that unhappiness seemed to be nothing more than a waiting room for fulfillment. Those days were hopeful, wrapped gently around with lapping waters. Now he believed his every step advanced a barren desert—his thirst called out to dry, empty places, his ears detecting a distant withdrawing roar.

Furtively plundering the classics of rape, the final catastrophe was coming to realize himself to be an imposter of a victim. He had no business comparing himself to some poor lass who had been beaten about the breasts and impaled. There was simply no denying it—he'd not been entered, nor had he entered. And even if he had been or had, it would not have been the same. There could be no book for what had happened to Taftly, and he, by god, would not be indecent enough to try and write one.

After days of this, days of suffering and believing he was responsible for his suffering, followed by days of believing that he shouldn't even complain since his suffering was hardly suffering when compared to the suffering of real victims, after days of hating himself and his pallid organ, and nights of self-loathing and horror, Taftly understood that he must obtain forgiveness. Whether or not he was to blame, whether or not he had actually suffered, whether or not anything had happened at all, he must be cleansed of himself. His new lean self had been damaged, and he could not run it away.

III

TAFTLY WONDERED IF SOMETHING CATHOLIC was called for. Perhaps his mauling required a special service in Latin, or some relic touching and holy water. There may even be a saint for such a calamity, Taftly thought, though he hoped not, really. He decided to locate a priest, be cleansed and then return to the Baptist church of his youth.

Saint Paul's looked like a barn mistakenly done up in stucco with a cross at its top instead of a weathercock. As Taftly walked through the sanctuary, he experienced pleasant fissures of trepidation. He was examining votive candles when Father Stevens emerged from a back door and charged down the aisle.

"They're bombing my office just now," Father Stevens said, offering Taftly a pew. "Roaches."

Taftly did not know priests had Southern accents. Father Stevens had a nice one and Taftly wondered if a Southerner could ever become pope. For a man who faced weirdness by spitting into his palm and groping his spectacles, Father Stevens seemed kind and knowledgeable. Taftly told him everything but the Clydesdales' names.

"My God. Dear me. We just don't have a special service. Good God. Really?"

Taftly nodded.

"But you didn't actually—"

Taftly cut him off, unable to endure the word actually. Nor did he want to hear the question. . "I don't think so," he said, shifting on his hands.

"You don't think so? You either *did* or *didn't,* son."

"I didn't. I couldn't. I wouldn't. But later, it seemed that I had. It felt so."

"Both of them?"

Taftly nodded. "I have terrible dreams about it."

"I expect so." Father Stevens started to laugh then caught himself. "Well, there's counseling, of course. You could say a 'Hail Mary,' though she might be the last person you'd want at this point."

"No, no. I feel I've actually—" Taftly flinched when the hated word tumbled from his mouth, something Father Stevens took to be a nervous tick brought on by the calamity. "I feel I've been granted a better understanding of women. Not evil women. I mean, obviously, them, too. But I feel very tender toward good women and what they go through some-times. I just need some kind of official blessing now, to get rid of the bad feelings." Taftly stared down at his shoes. He could not feel his feet in them, and they looked to be gag shoes belonging to a clown. "I feel like I'm one of the bad women."

Father Stevens shook his head, sighing. "I wish there were a service for you," he said, though he was in fact greatly relieved that there wasn't.

"Could you just make one up?" Taftly pleaded. "Couldn't you splash me with holy water? Or hyssop, could we dip hyssop in something and anoint me with it? What about flagellation? Should I be ordered to tear my hide with some device you have in back?"

"But you haven't done anything wrong. It's the others—those two bitches. Excuse me, but they should be beaten, whoever they are. They should be throttled until their eye-teeth rattle."

Taftly went soft in his pew.

Father Stevens ached for him. "Stand up!" he ordered. He made the sign of the cross and shoved Taftly's forehead with the butt of his palm the way the healers did on television, sending Taftly over the pew. It seemed appropriate and Taftly felt better instantly. He thanked Father Stevens and headed for First Baptist.

Pastor Bates was a "once saved, always saved" variety of believer, and Taftly's return was not a surprise to him. The part about Taftly being humbled threw him, however, and he stared at Taftly, one eye growing larger, the other diminishing, per his reputation. He stood well over six feet tall and tossed

Bible verses into the congregation like grenades. The swelling and shrinking of his eyes alone had reached many a lost soul.

"Dear boy, that's truly—*truly*—depraved."

"I know."

"You're an educated man, have you ever heard of anything similar?"

"Never," Taftly told him.

"They're not even sodomites, technically. They're, why they're stealth, moving just under the moral radar into a whole new decrepitude, but clearly—*clearly*—vile. You couldn't have known. God bless you. Welcome. Are you sane, er, safe. I mean, are the attackers still about?"

Taftly would not reveal the Clydesdales' names to Pastor Bates, either. He looked the big man over and grew ashamed. Here was a fellow who never would have allowed himself to be compromised. Taftly was short himself, not even five-eight, and he realized he had fended off many malcontents throughout his life simply because of his width. Having made himself delicate, he'd become easy prey. It hurt his feelings. The entire production had been about preparing himself for a gentle woman, yet he'd almost been forced into congress with the Clydesdales. In larger days, he would have treated them in the manner to which they were accustomed, giving them the back of his hand in a series of discrete but jaw-cracking volleys.

"We thought we lost you to learning," Pastor Bates was saying.

"Everything I learned made me sad. I believed everything. It hurt my feelings."

"Vanity," said the pastor.

"Yes, and if you can believe everything, what does it mean?"

Pastor Bates smiled. "But you're home at last."

"I hope so," Taftly said. Suddenly his belly touched the cold of his belt buckle and alarmed him. Had he become fat again? Had the Clydesdales made him pregnant somehow, injecting him with fatty eggs that would swell out no matter how much he ran or dieted? Could there be a germ of filth circulating his vital privates, waiting for the moment to catch hold and swell up into something unwanted? Would he have to labor over their grotesque spawn by yielding to an unwieldy paunch?

"Pastor?"

"Yes."

"I feel so bad in my stomach. Nauseated. Like morning sickness."

Pastor Bates said a longish prayer in the King James language, during which Taftly peered down and determined he was the same size as before, though he still feared he was in some terrible way pregnant. One thing had become certain, it would have to be a woman to tell him he was clean. A woman would have to accept and love him for him to believe he was all right again. Eventually, their affection growing apace, Taftly would require that she inspect him, though this would come much later. Finally, he would have to be handled, maybe even swallowed whole and lovingly. He meant this last to occur without perversion. Fending off words such as suck and gobble, he imagined himself simply being loved to the point of his dream girl needing to mouth him. This would be a sure sign he wasn't tainted.

And so he began to search for his dream girl again, in church and at the tavern. He repented of the many books he'd read, the paper idols. He recanted them. They were as nothing, nothing at all to him now, the shape he was in. What did Tolstoy have for a man whose pole had nearly been waxed by 450 pounds of heifer? In all his studies there'd not been a single line to rescue him from this debacle. He walked and prayed for miles, but fear and cotton-mouth persisted. At his mother's grave, deep in solitude, he would against his will recall the guilty hardness of his tool, seemingly so anxious to be fleeced of life. Women, when pillaged, went dry, but he had manifested the ability to perform admirably, something the twins had noticed before he'd managed to buck them. And the Clydesdales had been ravenous with him, jostling and squealing about all the pleasure he was going to give them whether he wanted to or not.

"You hard," Trixie had managed. Drool escaped her lips, and her breath visited Taftly in seven-course fashion. She'd had a go at something that was a carrier for pepperoni recently. There'd been garlic, too, and the hot rum. "Oh, you hard, little bitty! I believe you 'bout to join us back in the big leagues!" she'd cried.

IV

WHEN TAFTLY'S DREAM GIRL WALKED into the bar, he
was in the rest room. He'd not quite made it in time, as a matter of fact, and had erupted vehemently, splattering the edge of
the urinal and so his trousers. Fighting pregnancy, he'd been
running more than ever, and his bladder had become tyranni-
cal. He weighed very little and had crunched his way into abs
of steel. His brown hair, once thick and curly, had thinned a little on account of calorie deprivation, but with such assets as a
goatee and ripped khakis, he looked something like a starving
poet on the lam from a noble family heritage.

The bad thing about the khakis being shredded, however,
was that sometimes—this particular occasion, for instance—
urine misted his knee caps. He wiped with a paper towel,
grumbling. Really, Taftly thought, everything below the belt
has been permanently fouled. It was the Clydesdales' fault—he
hadn't seen the sluts in months—yet his anger got the better of
him, and he walked toward the bar accusing his dream girl that

he hardly believed in anyway, whoever she was, wherever she was, nameless and late as always. What a shock when Taftly saw her.

She looked nothing at all like he'd imagined, which he took to be the very best sign since in all his musings he'd never formulated anything as perfect as he longed for. Pitched over the bar at a provocative angle—but innocently—she was questioning Charlie the bartender about something. Her age looked to be that of a college senior quite a few years out of college, a nice trick Taftly believed. It was October, yet she wore a spring dress, a sheer cotton marvel, notable for its narrow shoulder straps and its generous offering of thigh. There was a little stringy leather bracelet around her wrist and a dear silver cross necklace. Such was her covering, a poised if simple ensemble if ever Taftly had seen one.

Long in the leg, she had a remarkable rear. Sometimes the girls with the great glorious legs were cheated in that department. Not so for Taftly's prize. And what's this? Breasts! Both of them ripe as if readied for suckling! Hurrah! Hurrah, hooray, thought Taftly, before taking note of his dream girl's wild confusion of golden hair that had been pinned up but tumbled down here and there to his deep satisfaction. Taftly drew close and took a seat, to be certain of her face.

It was exactly what Taftly had tried to have in mind but had never been able to get a clear picture of. His day dreams had traded drearily in lineaments and profiles. Here was the true flesh of it, though some refinements were unexpected. For instance, he'd surmised it would be best if his girl had green eyes, brightly aflame, the better to charge his battery, as his father had once put it before dying, leaving town. But this *real* dream girl had eyes that were taken from a different page entirely. They were brown and melting, wounded somehow, and very kind. Likewise, he'd suspected his girl would possess high cheek bones and a sort of squarish, oblong face, of the kind made popular lately by runway models. Instead, there was a stark nudeness to her round face, the face of a madonna on her wedding night. Her cheeks were blushed a little, even over the summer tan she had yet to surrender. Her eyebrows were light and sun splashed. There was something alarmingly feminine about this face, so unlike a man's, so unstrained and peeled of pretense, so accepting and wide with beauty. She seemed to have sprung upward from another realm, serene and yet furiously present, freshly arrived in the manner of Botticelli's Venus. Undressed of lipstick, her lips were fairybook red and hugely languorous, given to refreshing little twitches where they met in the warm wet corners of her mouth. Of course, he'd only just begun to observe her, and details were unreliable. Certainty would require proximity, minute measurements, all of his senses careening with stimulation.

"I'm sorry, Fay," Charlie was saying.

"Charlie, please."

Charlie polished a glass, his eyes tormented by the line of conversation. "Get away from him, Fay. You've been through enough already," Charlie told her.

"But Charlie. That's what I'm trying to do. Please. I have to talk to him. I *have* to. It's like he thinks he can get away with anything and he can't. He just can't."

Charlie stared at her. He was angry. Taftly knew he loved her too much and that she was trouble to love. Taftly was overcome with compassion for Charlie and with hatred for the man Fay, his dream girl, had to talk to. As soon as Taftly discovered the man's name, he'd go home and get his pistol and load it to the hilt. Well, damnit, he would.

"Well, what? Well what, Charlie?"

It was hard on Charlie and Taftly to see her importuning like that. Her role in life was to never be denied anything and somehow this unknown-to-Taftly motherfucker was making it necessary to turn Fay down.

"Well, no, I don't know where he is. But if I did—"

Charlie stopped talking. Tears were on the way to Fay's eyes. A great humanitarian longing burst from Taftly's lower intestine and swept his heart. Fay tried to smile but couldn't. She left the bar calmly and with dignity, but Taftly saw a host of cherubims trailing her, scowling. Someone would have to pay for this. Things sometimes went wrong, sure, but God didn't permit this kind of shit, original sin or no.

At that very moment, Taftly received another glimpse of the Total View and again knew how God saw him. He was being asked to do something beyond even the romantic, about that he was fairly certain. His near rape had only made him more willing and humble. Perhaps without it, he'd have sought some verification from his dream girl first, some loving act to quench his heart. But as a recent victim, he'd acquired nobility. He wasn't celibate, but he had his priorities. Fay needed understanding and someone to stomp the puke out of the man she claimed to have to talk to—Fay needed someone to be very Christian in her life. That very Christian person was Taftly Harper.

"Who was she?" Taftly asked.

"Fay. Fayceile," Charlie told him. "She's the prettiest. And the sweetest. It was Rodney Train she was after."

"*Train?*" Taftly blurted, incredulous and fearful. Train was a tremendously bad fellow, the only redneck to have ever worn a mood ring and sandals and survived it. He was slight but quick to fight. By always having a lot of dope on hand, he kept himself necessary, dealing mainly to the college kids. It was rumored he would sometimes make the girls pay out by way of degrading oral transactions, even if they had the money. Of course, Train started these rumors and was a proven liar.

"Women like Train. At first. He's real sweet to women. At first. Then he goes back to being Train."

Charlie wasn't happy about it, either. He'd gotten older and against this morbid progress had groomed a ponytail, which seemed to droop now with the news of Train. In truth, the ponytail did nothing to make Charlie look younger and he knew it, but then again, he would not ever have to be mistaken for an attorney. Charlie was scraggly mainly, and quiet.

There was supposed to be a plastic pipe behind the bar and Charlie, it was said, had filled it with cement, a rough trick learned from his groovy days spent down in Daytona Beach. Someone had the idea that Charlie had been a close friend of Greg and Duane Allman, that they'd ridden Harleys together when not otherwise busy scoring trim and grass. Because Charlie never bragged about it, everyone became convinced it was absolutely true.

Taftly thought of it again—Charlie loved Fay too much. It was the ideal occupation Taftly had been called unto, unto which he had been born. All his life he was in transit to this very task.

"I don't know much about Train except that I despise him," Taftly announced. He'd never said anything as surly in his life. All his days of spouting philosophy were zero compared to the thrill of it. This Fay was making a man of him already. It felt quite wonderful.

With the next sip of bourbon, Taftly's heart gone out toward the rescue and reward of Fay, a terrible vision besieged him: Trixie, mouth agape, mounted to the hilt on his thruster. Another: Trixie and Trina twisting his pork stallion like a flag-pole on May Day. Pagans! Pagan Wenches! Taftly begged God not to allow their dirty work to disqualify him.

"Know what Train did?" Charlie asked.

Taftly jerked back.

"Broke her jaw. What I heard." Charlie levelled his eyes and leaned close. "If it's true, if I find out, I believe something will happen to him one night."

Taftly was a veteran of abuse, a graduate of the dread school. As a man who had endured a rather prolonged attempted double rape, he was alert to infractions. He knew instantly that Train had brought Fay low by cracking her face. He smelled it. It was an event from the darkling world the Clydesdales had dragged Taftly into, and he felt almost privileged for having almost been made to service the two sows. When Taftly finally earned the right to love Fay, she'd find him knowing and understanding. Distinguished by tragedy, he would be unlike all the others. He could hardly wait.

Over the next few days, Taftly became hyperventilated about all the work to be done, like meeting Fay, learning her last name, wooing her and breaking up Train's skull. He drank coffee, took vitamins and fed hollow points to his pistol, spinning the chamber repeatedly and imagining the good fun he would soon be having when he got ahold of the devil's rump-bred harasser.

After a winning twelve-mile run one afternoon, he determined he was ready to return to the bar. A band was warming up which meant there would be students around. It wasn't the atmosphere Taftly wanted. And anyway, how did he know Fay would be there? He'd somehow managed to have never seen her before. Such bad luck could pick up where it left off and continue.

By nine o'clock Taftly was slightly drunk and defeated. He skipped out on his tab simply by virtue of being depressed and began to walk home. Passing the grocery store, he heard a ruckus in the back parking lot. He looked over and could not believe what he saw. It was Fay and Train. Fay was crying and Train was cursing out the window of his big black Chevy Tahoe, using the word whore a lot.

Taftly was afraid of Train, but he was more afraid of what his life would be like if he slinked away. Maybe God would only give him this one opportunity. "Damnit," he hissed. "It was easier being a goddamned atheist." God was very shrewd about the Total View, Taftly surmised. He didn't much let Taftly in on it, just enough to keep him yearning for a heroic Taftly.

Something pressed against Taftly's toes at that point. It happened to be a cement block and there could be no doubt about what to do with it. Rodney Train had become weary of berating Fay and was pulling out of the parking lot. The back of Train's Tahoe looked like Taftly's miracle waving goodbye to him. Taftly charged it, heaving the block through the rear window. Steeped to the gills on some fashionable hallucinogen, Train was instantly delivered into a brutal nightmare. He believed a rather large pit bull had taken a bite out of his vehicle. Having concluded that everything but the engine and the front seat had been devoured, he sensed his one chance of survival was to punch the gas and scream loudly. This he was in the process of doing when the sheriff pulled up in front of him.

"Come on," Taftly whispered.

Fay was so stunned by Taftly's boldness she immediately followed after his voice. They slipped down a side street, placid with oak and pecan trees. Down the way, there was music and laughter. Taftly had Fay's hand without thinking of it and suddenly realized he'd driven to the bar and had not needed to walk home at all except to fulfill God's will. Everything seemed very simple and clear to him.

"Let's get to my car," Taftly said.

"Okay," Fay said. But she stopped walking. "Wait, I think I know you. You're Taftly Harper. You were bigger, weren't you?"

"Once," Taftly said. "Come on."

"I knew your sister."

"I don't have a sister," Taftly told her. He greatly hoped his dream girl would not turn out to be stupid. Though he had no plans to become an intellectual again, his dream girl was supposed to be reasonably keen.

"I guess there's not another Taftly. Taftly Harper. Didn't your grandfather own the college or something? I got one of those Copiah Harper academic scholarships."

Taftly wanted to change the subject. He did not want Fay to continue connecting the old fat Taftly with the new superior version. "What's your last name?" he asked.

"Train," she said.

"What?" Taftly stopped.

"Haven't you heard the rumors? Rodney Train's been going around telling people we're married and that I'm pregnant. He even called up my pastor back home and told him that I'd walked out on him and wasn't living up to my conjugal obligations. Now he's telling people I'm planning to get an abortion. The son-of-a-bitch."

"My god." whispered Taftly.

"Yep. I'm afraid it's true. He's actually convinced people I'm carrying his baby. Can you imagine going around having to deny such a thing?" Fay retrieved a pack of clove cigarettes from her tiny purse. She lit one and tapped her foot. "I used to not smoke," she said. "I used to go to church and be a good person. I used to do a lot of things." She smiled and rolled her eyes. They were thoroughly exotic in the softness of the street light. "Damnit, after everything, I just can't believe this is happening."

Taftly noticed she had a faint lisp such as newcomers to braces have, a slight thickness with words.

"Train's an asshole," Taftly said.

Fay sighed. "You don't know the half of it." She gave Taftly a tough and sarcastic shrug, which Taftly respected, yet he had the uncomfortable feeling she would burst into tears at any moment. "Anywho, my name's Fay Davis. Davis like the president."

They took the next block and found Taftly's car. It was an embarrassment on a night like this one, an unheroic riceburner and he was ashamed of having to put Fay in it. *Consumer Reports* should have a category for degrees of emasculation, because Taftly's Jap two-door deserved a bad rating. It looked like something Train's big black Tahoe might shit up mindlessly while knocking down scenic miles. He could not look at Fay simply for this reason and opened her door with his eyes averted. But as he walked around behind the car—so as not to give her a view of him in his shame—he was buttressed by the fact that Fay had actually waited for him to open her door, a real lady. He thought of the Davis bit, too. She'd turned up the moist corners of her mouth when she'd said it, spoofing along as if the great Confederate were inches away.

They drove by the grocery. Fay wanted to, and Taftly was glad to do it because it turned out Train, the sheriff, or maybe Train's steering wheel had arranged for Train to get a broken nose. When they saw him, Fay put her hand to her lips. He was saying something about his wife leaving him and being pursued by a giant attack dog. The sheriff appeared very itchy with his billy club, as if Train needed a touch-up job for his face. Taftly hoped the ride to the station would be hard on Train. The sheriff could make it difficult, and from the looks of things he probably would.

"Where do you want me to take you?" Taftly asked. He concentrated on the road but had the peculiar feeling he was getting wide again, seeping over into the passenger's seat. His skin felt breathed on.

"Oh, I don't know. Anywhere."

"What about a drink?"

"But not anywhere public. I don't want to see anybody now."

"We could go to my place," Taftly suggested.

"Okay. But could you answer me one question. What the hell were you doing back there?"

"I hate your husband," Taftly told her.

"Very funny. So do I. Oh, you just wouldn't believe it if I told you," Fay said.

V

TAFTLY HAD SOME BOURBON AT HIS HOUSE, a premium brand from his days of reading. He brought it out and made them cocktails of bourbon and coke and lime, an odd twist but Taftly perceived it was called for.

"Now I know how I know you. I remember you from those philosophy society meetings they had on Thursday nights. I was a freshman. I'd go just to get extra credit in Dr. Wilson's logic class," Fay said. Taftly handed her a glass. "You probably never saw me. I sat in back and never said anything. But *you! You* were so *smart!* I had a crush on you. I bet you didn't know that."

Taftly coughed at this and wiped his mouth. "Me?" he said.

"Yes. I watched you. You were this cute little ball of a boy. You always wore one of those vests and everything you said was intelligent. You looked like a little Chesterton."

This was too much. Taftly's dream girl knew Chesterton? What Chesterton looked like and thought Taftly looked like him? "You know Chesterton?"

"He's my father's favorite. My father never cared for him becoming Catholic, but I had to read *Orthodoxy* when I was fourteen," Fay said. "You'd like my father."

"What does your father do?"

"He's a doctor. What about yours?"

"Oh, nothing much. He died. Left town. Died and left town. Or vice versa."

"I'm sorry." Fay rubbed Taftly's hand. "For whatever happened or didn't happen to him."

Fay was more beautiful than Taftly had thought, and he'd thought the world of her from first sight. He sat there, dazzled by her softness. Even her sarcasm was accommodating. She was the kind of person who hated to see people in pain. A shudder ran through him when he thought of what that would get you with a man like Rodney Train.

"I love whisky too much." Fay said. "I had a crazy uncle who was the same. He hijacked a plane once with his finger. You know, stuck it in his coat pocket and said it was a gun. They had to land in Shreveport. They were going all the way to Dallas. He thought because it was only his finger that he wouldn't get into trouble. But after they made an emergency landing, well, he found out differently."

Fay smiled directly into Taftly's eyes, something Botticelli's canvas Venus could never do. He'd done Fay wrong by comparing her to a painting. Things were clearer now. He noticed her teeth. They were almost too perfect. She was tying her hair back and becoming studious. All the best women could change like that. Taftly felt proud.

"Listen," Fay said. "What you did back there, for whatever reason, it was brave. My daddy would have loved to have seen that one, boy. And John—" She stopped and tilted back to keep from crying, fanning her eyes. "None of this would have happened if John—" She had to stop again. Taftly sat quietly, wondering if John was the great love of her life. He was going to ask when she said, "My brother. I can't talk about it."

"Sure," Taftly said, nodding encouragement.

"But Rodney Train has ruined my life, let me assure you."

Taftly scooted closer. He was having to convince himself not to tell Fay of his plans to marry her.

"It really was sweet," Fay was remarking. "Most people are afraid of Rodney."

Taftly wanted to tell her he wasn't afraid because he simply loved her too much and because God had given him a peek at the Total View. He wanted to get to the part where they shared tragedies and understood they were meant for one another.

"You know what? I've seen you running, too. Rodney and I passed you once, and he was going to throw a beer bottle at you—that's his idea of fun—but I stopped him. I should've let him. Obviously you would have kicked his ass."

Fay winked, and she and Taftly giggled. "You're the one that's sweet," Taftly said.

"I used to be a lot sweeter." Fay quit laughing.

"Tell me the whole story," Taftly said. It came out in the new authoritative way of speaking he'd just gotten the knack of.

"Maybe I should," Fay said. "I've never told anyone. I need to tell somebody."

She stood and went to the kitchen for more ice, arriving even nearer to Taftly's side with a momentous seriousness. Taftly was struck with a vile notion—how could Fay be as wonderful as she was and yet be willing to sit here with Taftly Harper? He fought the thing off, the double-edged insight that diminished the both of them. It was the kind of thinking that had kept him lonely all his life. Besides, it was their fate to overwhelm past devastations. It was exactly what would make them better, what would secure and make sturdy their bliss.

"Some friends of mine were buying dope from Rodney," Fay began. "That's how it all got started. I'm not a user. But they thought he was cute and I guess he saw me and told them he'd give them a discount if they introduced us. We were at a party at this house outside of town. He was cute in a redneck way, I guess, kind of tight jeans and T-shirt, absolute trash, but very polite. You know what's funny? My first impression of him. I thought he was the most naive little boy in the world. Me! A virgin!"

"A virgin?" Taftly had not meant to blurt this but waited anxiously for an answer nonetheless.

"Yes. It happens when you don't have sex. I managed four years of college like that and then ran into Train. Oh, I fooled around and all, but you know, never actually did it. I was waiting to get married. Rodney Train was the perfect way not to accomplish that. I didn't know anything about him. He just seemed like a sweet boy. He acted shy but asked me out first thing. My daddy's like that and I'm partial to it. Like me coming to your house because you threw a block through Train's window, see? Anyway, we went to the Peking Duck. He claimed to read poetry. He could only name Robert Frost but it was still cute, that he tried like that. Well, two or three dates later I'm realizing we really have no business going out together and he's getting heated up. So he begs for one more date. We drive out to his place and he pulls out a joint. I was never afraid around him because he was always very, how should I describe it, well, proud, sure, he was proud of my virginity. Sometimes people don't believe you're a virgin. He assumed since I hadn't slept with him I *had* to be a virgin. Typical egomaniac, right? But when he found out I really *was* a virgin, that was it. He was in awe of it. Do you mind if I smoke? I'm quitting."

Taftly joined her this time. He'd learned to smoke profoundly during his coterie days and thought Fay should see just how effective he was with a cigarette. She would know what to make of the information.

He'd never handled cloves before and thought they smelled lovely. The crackling they did was a joy. They were strong, too, and after drawing a few times Taftly felt the top of his head begin to unlatch, something that was not at all unpleasant.

"Okay, he lights up and says kiss me and then of course he shotguns me and holds my mouth shut. We were giggling and I stomped hell out of his foot and it became a little game, him shotguning me with kisses." Fay was smiling the way people smile when they recall a lost dog or salad days. "Good-by kisses he called them. And then, right in the middle of it, he just breaks down and a starts sobbing. I mean bawling. How he loves me. How he's going to miss me. How he's not good enough for me. I was having trouble following him at that point. Time was kind of bending around. I hated to see him in that much pain, and I started to think he was going to die. Really. I was high and didn't even know it. Or didn't understand it at least, what all it can do to you."

Fay clicked her perfect teeth. Taftly knew a sordid revelation was forthcoming. He believed he would make her feel better with his own. Trouble was, his head was becoming unmanageable and he feared someone may have laced Fay's cloves with an illegal substance.

"I probably shouldn't be telling you this," Fay said.

"But you said you needed to. I have something to tell, too. Something that happened to me that was terrible. Please," Taftly pleaded. "Please go on."

"You look like you're going to cry," Fay said. She smoothed his cheeks. They were atremble.

"I just want you to be able to tell it," Taftly said.

"All right," Fay said. "You've been so kind."

"I want to be like Jesus," Taftly told her. "It's why I lost weight."

This was a complete lie and Taftly could not believe it had come out of his mouth. Fay sensed it and began to laugh. They both were laughing.

"Jesus was many things, but fat he wasn't," Fay said.

"Neither form nor comeliness," Taftly allowed. "Comeliness is actually a pretty cool word."

"*Cool?* Comeliness is *cool?*"

When the laughter wore out, Taftly looked at Fay with a painful tenderness. Fay gathered his fingers as if each of them demanded much careful attention. "I shouldn't be here, Taftly. I'm not good for you."

"You don't even know me. You just met me. How do you know what's good for me?"

"No, I'm right," she said, stroking his fingers. "I know me. I'm not in a good place right now."

"Why don't you finish what happened and let me decide," Taftly announced.

"Let you decide?"

"Yes. Let me decide. You owe me that much."

"I suppose I do. You got even for me. Wow. Sheriff Williams. He was pissed. It's going to be a long night for old Rodney Train, that's for sure. But he deserves it. He's handed out a few long nights in his day."

Fay put Taftly's fingers back on the olive green shag carpet where she'd found them. She looked away. Though she was already drunk, she planned on becoming more so, especially if she was going to tell about her and Rodney Train. An imperative had been handed down: She'd been treated kindly by the kindly Taftly Harper and now must tell him everything. She really had been very enthusiastic about Taftly once. He was someone from her days of innocence, someone she'd admired. Taftly Harper—what a swell name. And losing all that weight, gosh what an accomplishment, because he'd been pretty rotund after all. Taftly, Taftly. the night is closing in on us, we are alone, adrift from every shore. It is no time of life for secrets. How could a man who would go to the extreme of pitching a concrete block through Rodney Train's window be denied anything? Answer that, Fay? Fay *Train*. The answer is that he cannot be.

A bittersweet melancholy swept the room for both of them. They were nostalgic for a past they did not have. Both of them thought of what might have been and longed for it. They continued drinking quietly, settling things. Taftly stretched his legs out. Fay sighed. She believed she was ready to get the story out once and for all.

VI

"RODNEY'S VERY MANIPULATIVE," Fay said softly, pulling at strands of shag carpet. "He may seem like a dumb redneck, but believe you me, he's very clever. That night, he sat in a corner, crying, telling me to get out of his house, because he loved me so much it hurt him to be around me. Of course, I went over to him, just as he expected. I tried to comfort him but he began pushing my head down. I thought I could at least, you know, put my head in his lap if that would make him feel better. Everything was happening so fast, and I hated him crying like that. I felt very guilty. I thought I'd done something terrible to him and that I owed him. The truth is, I feel that way a lot. My problem is I like men, *really* like them, and I think it's hard to get along with men if you really like them. I like doing things for them and being with them. I love them. But I don't think that's the way you should be. You know why? I hate to beat a dead horse half to death or whatever that saying is, but not every man is like a girl's daddy.

They always talk about bad fathers, right, but they never talk about what a really great father can do to you. Or a great brother for that matter. They make you think men are one way, *their* way, when sometimes they're another way, *Train's* way, do you see?"

Taftly nodded, heartbroken. He was along her father and brother's lines, but knew that now was not the time to explain it.

"Well, you can imagine what happened. He kept forcing me down there and then he took himself out and made me. The whole time I was cutting little deals with myself, like just kiss it or just do it for a second, you know, trying to find a way to make him stop crying and to get out of there. But then he wasn't crying and he had me by the hair. And then he was rough and *I* was crying. The tables turned so quickly. One minute I'm taking pity on *him*, worried about *him*, and the next he's forcing me to do that to him and talking crude and jerking my head up and down. He knew it was coming all along. So to speak. That son-of-a-bitch."

The ceiling seemed to descend somehow and Fay closed her eyes. She knew she was crying because Taftly made a pained noise and dabbed her with a handkerchief.

"I got sick afterwards and maybe even a little hysterical and he was crying again, too, apologizing, saying he really loved me, that he'd never felt like that about any of the other girls he'd date raped. He didn't put it like that obviously, but it's the truth. Anyway, so much for my virgin high. Can I have another drink? A strong one?"

Taftly quickly rose to make the next round. There was a photograph of him and his mother on the refrigerator. It did a number on him and he took it and placed it in the freezer behind a stack of pot pies.

Fay was already talking when he walked back into the living room. Her cheeks were glazed with tear streaks and she was smoking again. "You know how time kind of blurs when you're messed up?" she asked.

"Of course," Taftly said. His vest and three-button suit group had gone a long month on very little besides Coleridge and hemp. One of the group had produced a shotgun at some point and they'd blown a lamp shade to bits, believing it to be an albatross. Taftly knew all about things blurring.

"Well, that was happening. With a vengeance. But for me, no one had explained it would happen, and so I started thinking Rodney had damaged my brain, you know, with his—" Fay shrugged demurely and made a face. Taftly nodded and she continued. "I mean, he'd been so rough with me and I started to think maybe my mouth was bleeding. I tried to run out of the house. The next thing I know, he's caught me from behind and I'm fighting and I feel him, you know, *feel* him, against the back of my legs. I was really fighting now but it felt like I was underwater and then he'd gotten my skirt up and he was saying, Shit! Oh, shit! I guess he'd been premature. It was degrading, but it kept me from getting raped. I later learned he had a thing about rape and it got him so worked up that he was premature a lot. No telling how many girls it saved. In some ways, I guess the bastard was a failure as a rapist."

"But he saw you?" Taftly demanded.

"My rear-end he did. Listen, that was the least of my problems."

Taftly accepted this. "I know. I'm sorry," he said.

"Oh, no. You're sweet. If I'd been going out with someone like you, none of this would have happened. I guess, basically, I'm an idiot to have ever gone out with Rodney Train in the first place."

Taftly took another cigarette and sent up a ring of smoke, imagining a few terrible things to do to Train. "Did you press charges?"

"No, I was too scared and embarrassed. And then everything just got worse. He took me home and I was up all night vomiting and praying that I wasn't pregnant, because I didn't know exactly what had happened and I was pretty paranoid. Well, guess who shows up the next morning with flowers? Rodney Train. I told him I never wanted to see him again, but he said we had to talk. He said he was in love with me and that I might be pregnant. He knew I was vulnerable to something like that. I hate him, Taftly. I hate him so much I can't just walk away. He can't get away with this."

Taftly lurched in her direction, then retreated. "I know, I understand," he told her.

"Anyway, so he says he wants to stand by me, at least until we knew for sure. He told me he was enrolling in medical school, taking that course that gets you ready for the entrance exams. What utter unadulterated bullshit. I mean, like I'm going to believe it or even care, you know?"

Taftly knew, all right. The medical school bit was deplorable and Train would suffer extra for it.

"Well, of all things, lo and behold, I skip my period. I made the mistake of telling my roommate and it got back to Train. He was euphoric, thrilled, and came over telling me we had to get married, that the baby had to have a father. I called the cops on him. He came back the next day and I called them again and got a restraining order. I was messed up bad, thinking I was carrying Train's baby, thinking I'd just slapped a restraining order on the baby's daddy. As it turned out, I wasn't pregnant, which meant, among other things, that I never had to see Rodney Train again. What a liar. He told me his sperm could seep down into me even if I wasn't penetrated, which he insisted I was. You can be smart and be an idiot, Taftly. You're looking at someone who had all the advantages and turned out to be a complete idiot."

"Don't say that. Train tricked you."

Fay shook her head. "Yeah. But it's also true that I'm an idiot. Anyway, when I found out that I wasn't pregnant and was still a virgin on top of it, I wanted to get rid of everything about Rodney Train. I somehow came up with the brilliant idea that the only way for me to be clean was to somehow reverse what had happened, to make it so that it wasn't really me being raped, because me being raped seemed like my fault.

I started going out and partying and thinking the way to do it was to get somebody to do what Rodney hadn't been able to, to teach him a lesson, to get rid of him like that. It was a bad time for me. Maybe it was worse than what happened that night with Rodney. Anyway, I lost my virginity, oh boy, did I ever, and after doing that, I got lost, period, for awhile, trying to take back what Rodney had taken away, when suddenly, one night, one nightmare night, I was with this guy when I suddenly realized it had been Rodney Train all along, that he'd gotten to me anyway, over and over again. And then what do you know but Rodney's going around telling people I'm having his baby or trying to get an abortion or whatever. Can you believe it? After all that, after everything. I mean, can you even believe it?"

VII

THE NEXT DAY THEY FOUND OUT TAFTLY had become a rather serious hero. Rodney Train had tried to attack the sheriff and took a beating for it. An awful lot of cocaine and heroin was discovered in his truck and he would be going to the penitentiary for a long while. All of which made Fay feel very sweet about Taftly. He found that all he had to do was ask and an entire evening could be his. They began to go for coffee and even did some shopping together. Though not exactly dating, Taftly believed they were coyly edging into the sphere of romance. The patient advance was in keeping with his longtime dream and he believed soon they would fall upon one another and speak directly of love.

Fay went home for a couple of weeks around Thanksgiving and Taftly could hardly abide it. He spent long nights at the Copiah Harper Tavern. Train made bail about this time and one night walked into the bar and whacked a beer bottle across the back of Taftly's head. Charlie subdued him with the legendary pipe, arranging wonders on Train's face. Charlie proved to have a touch of Picasso in him and worked feverishly until the sheriff stopped him. Taftly only had a concussion and could not wait to tell Fay.

But when Fay returned, Taftly saw that something had changed. His movements were a constant rushing toward Fay, yet she seemed more and more to merely lean into him with sad affection, as if she were making a buffer of her body and hiding something. Taftly stole kisses, but such thievery began to hurt his feelings. They went for long walks and found nothing at all to say. Leaves sailed down past them.

Taftly came to believe he needed to tell Fay about how he had suffered because of the Clydesdales. Fay was so devoutly earnest about soothing pain he knew she was, no matter what, his one true dream-girl. Her imperfections were the exact imperfections he required. She would need him to look after her in the coming years. Taftly would always be ready to make her love herself again as much as he would surely always love her. He estimated he was on the very heels of salvation. All that was left was for her to tell him she loved him, and then, of course, to make him whole through ministrations.

The second weekend in December, Taftly took her to the Catfish Cabin. Loaded down with a pint of bourbon, a jug of wine and two packs of clove cigarettes, he anticipated an evening that would speed them forward.

He knew he would have to be bold and tell her about the Clydesdales in a way that would not make her think him weak.

This seemed to be all but insurmountable, yet he believed that if the mood were right, he would know how to proceed. He also needed to shatter the friendship barrier. Their time together was tending toward the platonic. Taftly had never liked Plato anyway. Now he knew why.

At first, things seemed to be moving along nicely. They happened into a frantic conversation about country music that left them feeling closer to one another. They had agreed, passionately, about everything.

"I want you to be my girlfriend," Taftly announced. He'd hardly touched his catfish.

"Oh, Taftly. I'm spoiled. I'm not good enough for you."

Taftly slammed his hand down and tipped his wine glass. "No! Don't ever, ever say that!"

"Okay. I'm sorry. I'm sorry, Taftly. I just don't want to hurt you, that's all."

"I've had a recent trauma myself," Taftly said. "Not so recent anymore, but in my mind it is. I didn't mean to scare you. Don't cry. That's the last thing I want."

Fay went over and sat on Taftly's side of the table. The simple charm and decency of this act overwhelmed him. "Thanks," he said.

"This is how the European couples sit," Fay said. She took his hand like a lover and Taftly's desperate heart revived. "They never sit across from each other. It's too far. It is, isn't it?"

"I think so," Taftly said.

"Tell me what happened to you?"

"I don't know," Taftly was afraid of ruining the moment.

"Come on."

"Some people got carried away and—"

He could not tell her. They would have needed twenty years of marriage, grandchildren and a bucket of quaaludes to handle the news. Taftly was certain now that his story about being used would make Fay feel unsafe around him.

"And what?"

"I got robbed. Bad."

"Really?"

"Yes. And I had to shoot somebody in the back because of it."

"What? Really?"

"Yes. It was unfortunate. May I kiss your mouth?"

Fay smiled. "Please do," she said, then leaned close and sort of dragged her juicy lips over Taftly's. He sent his tongue out, but she pulled away.

"I'm sorry. I'm self-conscious about my mouth."

"Because of Train?"

She nodded.

Taftly's eyes were awash with understanding. If only he could find a way to tell her about his ordeal, they had every chance of being able to heal one another. By placing his abused member into her abused mouth, he calculated their ruination would be canceled out, nullified. As soon as this thought crossed his mind, he wanted to slap himself unconscious for it. It seemed exceptionally vile to him, *Trainesque,* even, and he would perhaps do something painful to himself later that night to teach himself a lesson.

But then Fay was near him again, caressing his hand. There was a bouquet of cleavage there below and Taftly had the idea Fay's nipples would be very large and inflamed, like her lips, which pleased him. The thought seemed pure and good and he stayed with it. The Clydesdales, ironically, possessed tiny lips and were nippled with pale vanishing things.

"It's not fair," Fay was saying. "Nothing's fair."

After supper, they went to Taftly's house and brought out some candles. "You shouldn't be self-conscious about your mouth," Taftly said. "What he made you do doesn't even count."

"Oh, that's not what I meant," Fay told him.

Taftly looked over.

"He hit me here," Fay said softly. She tapped her lips like a little girl.

Taftly recalled Charlie saying Rodney Train had broken her jaw. "I'm sorry." He touched Fay's cheek.

Fay was becoming very sad. Taftly told her that she didn't have to talk about what happened. She was looking out the window when she began to trace something on Taftly's leg. It was a name, he thought, a long one, continuing far up his thigh.

She was crying when she turned to him. "Rodney Train's going to prison for a long time. Because of you. Because of you, Taftly. You did it. I want something for you that's wrong.

But I feel so bad inside that I can't imagine why it should matter, why you, of all people, should be denied it. It would be just another unfair thing. And that's not fair to you. Please, Taftly. Say I have to. Please, say I do. Say you want me to, Taftly."

She was inside his pants now and Taftly could not believe it. "Stop! My god, Fay! Stop it!"

"Make me. My whole life is over anyway. Make me, Taftly. It's not fair. Make me."

"Just love me, Fay. Let's love. Let's love each other. Is that too much to ask?"

"Oh, Taftly! It's not fair. Please don't talk about love to me. Just make me. Because I have to say good-bye, Taftly. I'm going to get married."

When she saw Taftly's eyes, the shock of pain in them, she began to cry even harder.

"He's an old friend. He's a doctor. And he's going to practice with daddy. It's just happening. I can't stop it. Taftly! Taftly, please! It's not fair for Rodney Train and those others to get what they got and you to get nothing! I'm too sick to love you! Just make me!"

Fay placed Taftly's hand atop her head, atop the very crown of his dreams. She curled his fingers into her hair. She hated herself and wanted Taftly to hate her too. She dropped to her knees before him on the couch. He was crying, tightening the clump of silken hair.

"Just love me," he pleaded. But already he realized it was impossible.

"Make me! Just make me."

"Shut up! Just shut up!" he cried.

Fay brought Taftly out, his old wound, and prepared to silence herself with it. Tears fled Taftly's eyes and he stared at the ceiling. He noticed Fay had done something strange with her mouth down there, something about her teeth, but he surrendered himself and closed his eyes. He sobbed for the duration and did not even watch her leave.

VIII

ON A COLD FEBRUARY NIGHT before Valentine's Day weekend, Taftly found the Copiah Harper Tavern filled with nicely dressed young professionals. Charlie told him it was a bachelor party. "That's Fay's fiance over there. They're getting married this weekend. Real nice fellow," Charlie allowed.

Taftly ordered a tall glass of bourbon and concentrated on the voices behind him. He looked over at the photograph of his granddaddy. The sea of enamel was peeling away rapidly now, leaving vacant chips all around the somber ancient face. The old man looked marooned and landlocked. For the first time Taftly thought he looked unhappy.

When the liquor hit, Taftly turned and stared menacingly at the bachelor party, but the revelers were too drunk to notice. The group was uniformly inferior in his estimation. He tried to locate Fay's brother amongst them but no one seemed to fit Taftly's idea of what Fay's brother might look like. It was just as well that he wasn't there with such hooligans, Taftly decided.

One of the group seemed older and somewhat out-of-sorts. Taftly tagged him as the fiance, but with the boozy commotion it was difficult to get a good take on his features. He looked to be about a minute or two from total eclipse and still the others were making him drink when suddenly one of his buddies said something that caused him to rally.

"*Has she ever taken them out for you?*"

"What's that?"

"Her bridge." The fellow chuckled, but went ahead. "Hey, all due respect, but, I mean, you've got to admit it's fascinating to think about getting gummed like that." He stopped now, his face scarred by a stiff shamed smile.

The young men were quiet and nervous and Fay's fiance seemed perplexed, driven to unwanted consideration. His brow wrinkled. Then he said, thoughtfully, "No. She's not done that. She won't ever. Period." After this. he leapt from his chair. He had landed several vicious blows to the top of his friend's head before Taftly walked out the door.

It was very cold outside and Taftly thought the town looked picked over because of the dark weather. The headlights of passing cars were painfully sharp in the crisp air. There were dead leaves fluttering about. Soon it would snow. His granddaddy had loved the town best when it was frosted. As a child, Taftly had taken rides with him in his Buick, looking at the fresh winter houses and trees. "Never forget Lee's men, Taftly," his granddaddy would insist. "They fought barefoot, in snow just like this. It sure wasn't pretty to them. It was cold and they were hungry. But the worst was they were *lonely*. I can just imagine it." His granddaddy meant this to be inspiring, but whenever Taftly recalled it, he was left shaken and believing something had gone wrong. He'd always thought that something was his father, but he sometimes suspected it may have been more than that. At last he thought he knew.

Taftly walked to the grocery and sat with his back against the cool bricks, staring out across the parking lot. A family approached a mini-van arguing, all of them clamoring for the last word. Once they had driven away, the grounds were quiet again and Taftly searched the grey sky. He imagined cement blocks tumbling down like manna, and of people running for cover and all the injuries.

So Fay had removed her teeth for him. Rodney Train had knocked them out and she'd had to get new ones that were too white and perfect and then she'd taken them out for Taftly. It was the best she could do and she would never do it again, not even for her husband, not even for Taftly.

He felt his belly sagging over his belt then and wished he were thin again. It had been a mistake to give that up. He longed to believe that the Total View was of him as a handsome Christian, but sometimes, more and more lately, Taftly believed it was too much to ask for.

PART
2

IX

SEVERAL YEARS LATER, shortly after Taftly's birthday—which his father had wickedly arranged to take place on April Fool's Day annually—the fear set in. It set in Taftly's teeth. At least that is where he first discovered it.

Having collapsed on his mother's crush-velvet plum-colored love seat after a rather chaotic encounter with a jump-rope and two twenty-pound dumbbells, Taftly perceived that his teeth had been transformed into receptors for doom. They were on edge, as if packed in ice, and highly sensitive. He wished they would simply revolt and crawl from his mouth, and it sometimes felt as if that were exactly what they were doing, attempting a panicky and poorly planned escape.

Sensing tragedy everywhere, Taftly tried to bite down on it. He sought to accomplish this by mumbling "catastrophe" over and over again. As his teeth had become peculiar, he pursued the word gingerly, though his face was given over to a terrific scowl. Catastrophe, he noticed, felt like hard candy, with minor casualties crumbling away like granules of rotten sugar.

Taftly recognized all of this as Fay's legacy. He believed it further degraded her, but there was nothing he could really do about it.

Within a week of discovering his teeth were clairvoyant or quite possibly metaphysically attuned, Taftly abandoned the love seat and put the house on the market. He thought his mother might want him to. In order to come to terms with his teeth, the Total View, or the lack of it, he required quiet acres in which to spend long days uncluttered with human contact or conversation. Having turned thirty-two but no wiser, he saw little reason for another round of seasons unless he knew exactly where he stood.

His life had become a preposterous exercise in witless persistence anyway. The night when he'd sat in the grocery store parking lot watching the snow fall he'd concluded that he'd come to the end of the story. But then he'd gone on living. Day after day he was still alive. Continuing like that struck him as unreasonable. When his teeth began to hector and alarm him, Taftly knew something had to be done and so hatched his plan to take to the woods and learn the truth of things once and for all.

He found just the place not ten miles from town, a handsome spread that could be had for a song. The property came with a quaint log cabin, a canning shed, a fishing pond, a dilapidated chicken coop and a handy man named Dennis Jolly, who lived in a deluxe shack on the other side of the pond.

The thing about Dennis, Taftly quickly discerned, was that he wasn't handy, was constantly rapping at the door to borrow money, could talk for hours on end without giving any pleasure and was possessed with a set of false chompers so sizeable that Taftly lay in bed at night slurping a mixture of lime jello and pure grain alcohol while wondering if the man had been fitted by a horse doctor. That Taftly had gone from Fay's teeth to the recent phenomenon of his own communicative molars was unsettling enough. But now, confronted with Dennis Jolly, the entire progression had taken on a thoroughly monstrous quality.

Nor was that all. It was hard to say how old Dennis was, or *why* he was. His essence, Taftly determined, was superfluity. He sometimes had the aspect of an invincible fortress of uselessness. Evolution could never account for Dennis Jolly. He seemed to have been a mistake of proportions that could only find explanation in the existence of a malevolent deity. Had Darwin discovered Dennis on one of the Galapagos Islands, he would have theorized his way into a suicide.

To make matters worse, Dennis couldn't go for more than a minute without decrying how the world had failed him, *him*, as if he were a deserving prince fiendishly stripped of his crown. Almost every time he opened his mouth it caused enormous pain to whomever happened to be within earshot.

"Earshot's goddamned right," Taftly once blasphemed after enduring a forty minute lecture on the shiftlessness of teen-age girls. According to Dennis, if the young minxes had had any class whatsoever, they would have been flocking to him in furious numbers. The only women who took to Dennis, Dennis alleged, were buxom wealthy housewives with advanced tastes and intelligence. There it was—he could only attract married women who were brainy and extremely beautiful, a real shame. Dennis always had news along these lines, and Taftly began to think of his words as shrapnel exploding from his terrible unrelenting teeth.

Dennis had lost most of his hair, too—a government experiment, he claimed. He wore a baseball cap pulled so low on his forehead it appeared to be a form of self-mutilation. Wedged severely inside the cap, his ears looked as if they'd been mauled during a dog fight. What is more, he cavorted about the property shirtless, wearing sheer running shorts and a fanny pack he'd been given by a lost European tourist.

"If you ever find me dead of exhaustion from working too hard, do me a favor," Dennis grandly announced one afternoon. He was reclining on his elbow, sipping an orange soda, something he'd been doing for about a week. "Bury me with this little baby," he said finally, patting the fanny pack and casting about with a fatigued expression.

How Taftly wanted to. How he wanted to bury Dennis with his fanny pack.

At least Dennis had this going for him—he had stories that made Taftly's Clydesdale experience seem almost petty, a thing Taftly had not thought possible. Dennis frequently claimed to have been abducted by aliens, for instance, and made to soil himself repeatedly in front of whole families of extra-terrestrials.

"Some kind of test?" Taftly asked, unable to simply walk away.

"Hell no!" Dennis blasted. "For entertainment. Sombitches made me shit on myself strictly for laughs. It was like I was a comedian. But in space."

Dennis's eyes, which resembled smokey marbles, bugged, as did, inevitably, his teeth. "That shit wadn't funny!" he cackled. His laughter was loud and stabbing, reaching Taftly like a barrage of lively slaps to the face. "Get it? Get it? That *shit* wadn't funny?"

Taftly attempted to achieve a safe distance from Dennis, but Dennis had sprung to his feet in the excitement and was pressing in. "And I'll tell you something else. Something private," he whispered, pointing his finger at Taftly's chest. "Laxative they gave me...*glowed in the dark.*" Dennis nodded direly. "That ain't all," he continued, his eyes wide with enthusiastic fright. "*It was a suppository.*"

Having once caught an episode of the "X-Files," Dennis rushed over to tell Taftly the real story: "They ain't listed under X."

Taftly trembled with rage. Dennis had brought this revelation to him at six in the morning, waking Taftly from a deep and needy slumber. "What the hell are you talking about?" he demanded.

"They're listed under Z. They're the Z files, not the X files.

You see how this could throw people off the scent, get everybody looking in the wrong place and what not?"

At that moment, Taftly realized that Dennis resembled a Pez candy dispenser, a shaft for a body and a big quick-action head. The only thing that made sense was the idea of beating Dennis into the ground like a tent stake and fetching a lawn mower to finish the job.

Yet as the months passed and spring thickened to summer, Taftly discovered something deeply unsettling. More than anything in the world, Dennis reminded Taftly of Taftly. Here at last was the embodiment of how Taftly felt about himself—here was the living proof.

Taftly felt sorry for Dennis because of this. He felt God had made Dennis for the express purpose of making Taftly aware of how wretched he was. It wasn't fair to Dennis. It wasn't fair to Taftly, either. And yet, Taftly sensed, they both deserved it.

Sometimes in the middle of Dennis's absurd harangues—Dennis's mouth gone frothy with excitement, tedious information and diatribes gushing from his trap like Old Faithful—Taftly would feel the sting of tears so tender and refined they scalded his cheeks.

What was happening could hardly be understood. Having gone into the woods in pursuit of himself, Taftly had instead become a ravenous maw for contradictions, paradoxes. He hated, loved everything, nothing. It was his blessing, curse to be so varied, divided. Once a master of intellectual empathy, he had against his will graduated into an extremely combustible state of intellectual, psychological and emotional sympathy. Formerly a sad song, he was being transformed into a terrifying symphony. Instead of just the one sorry Taftly, there were now many regrettable versions, all of them quite mouthy. In sum, Taftly felt as if he was vanishing by multiplication.

"It smarts," he'd point out.

"Yes, that's it, it smarts," he'd agree, snickering.

"But it really does. It's impossible."

"That's possible."

"Stop it!"

"Watch your tone."

"Oh, fuck you very hard, Taftly Harper!"

"Couldn't have said it better myself."

Taftly always got the best of himself in these arguments and believed things would never be any different. Pain, he decided, was not the worst thing in the world. What was worse was what he was tacking toward and it terrified him.

Perhaps he was to spend his remaining days drifting over a vast sea of anguish with no wind for his tattered sails, with no sextant or hope of landfall. He believed he could endure almost anything, but endure almost anything for *what*, toward what *end?* That was the question.

Snockered on Everclear and Jell-O—which he ladled into his gullet with a wooden spoon as if it were a special soup for his troubled soul—he'd grit his pestilent teeth and contemplate the pure pleasure of relieving himself of himself by loading up one of his guns and returning fire. The fact of the matter was thoughts of suicide kept him alive. If it had not been for the possibility of death, Taftly never would have made it.

This would have been ironic, but irony, Taftly was beginning to learn, required at least a veneer of meaning. Irony was a believer's game. When Taftly had sleeked down for his dream girl only to suffer a near-rutting by the hefty Clydesdales, that was ironic. When he'd actually found his dream girl only to discover that she'd experienced something along the same lines, that, too, was ironic. When she'd taken him toothlessly, their wounds mated at last, there was irony there as well, no question. And while each of these events was admittedly very bitter, they nevertheless shared one crucial quality—Taftly believed they amounted to something.

After Fay's marriage, on the other hand, he thought those things had happened for no good reason at all. The more Taftly thought of what had occurred, the less ironic it seemed. For without so much as a mustard seed's worth of faith, there was nothing for irony to latch hold of. Taftly believed he'd been worn too thin for purchase and had come a cropper.

Late at night, while puttering morosely about the house, he often longed for his mother. He wanted her to come back and take care of him. He wanted another chance to take care of her, too, and to dance big dances to the big bands and perhaps even wean her from saturated fats. He yearned for her prayers and her endless Bible readings, for the cold hard facts of her collapsed life right before him, facts which she stunned backwards with verses of scripture and her own tender singing.

Florence Harper had been a country beauty with enormous knockers and a trim waist-line until she began her losing battle with Little Debbie. She'd aspired to be educated and cultured—she'd aspired, as Taftly well knew, to Julius Harper, something it had been Taftly's duty to make up for.

According to Taftly, Taftly hadn't. "Exhibit A," he would announce, pointing toward the piano, recalling his mother's attempts to make a pianist of him. How Taftly wished he'd spent all of his days playing tunes for his mother. Life had been unkind to her and he'd had no right during childhood to skip lessons and play the dullard before the keys. Had he only listened to her he would be able to go into the living room where his mother's Steinway sat and finger his way through Beethoven's "Moonlight Sonata." She liked that one best but Taftly had only learned "Chop Sticks."

As a consequence, he often battered out maudlin variations of "Chop Sticks" until his fingers were numb. It was not uncommon for him to do so while wearing his mother's housecoat. On rainy summer afternoons, as his tin roof sizzled and snared and put him in the mood for music, he'd retrieve this ruined item. It had faded to the color of fresh vomit, its once silky texture hardened to near parchment. Around the neck of it curled a shedding frill of *faux* fur which seemed to be the imitation pelt of some whitened moon pup brought down to earth for slaughter. But as far as Taftly was concerned, the gown was snug comfort, and after finishing with the piano he'd stand and wrap his arms around himself to give his mother a hug. Eventually he'd be shaking and calling to her, looking like a lewd pimp ghost booted from the red-light district of some low-rent netherworld.

"Mama, mama—there's no one left but me and I'm not good company," he'd tell her, watching the lights swirl about him in uncertain do-si-dos.

It sometimes seemed that all that was left was "Chop Sticks" and books. He'd begun to read again, violently, arguing with the great philosophers and theologians and not infrequently pitching their books across the room. On one occasion he'd even thrown a volume to the floor and begun stomping it until the cover had torn free of its binding, after which he spat upon the title page for good measure.

That had been Nietzsche. During the days of his three-button-suit coterie, Taftly and the boys had considered Nietzsche an eloquent rebel and a fierce truth-teller. Now Taftly thought Nietzsche an arch liar and a coward. Anytime the house creaked or some random noise permeated the gloom, Taftly wished it was Nietzsche. He dared Nietzsche to show up and take the beating he had coming to him. *Like anyone could will anything to power after having been slobbered over by Clydesdales*, Taftly fumed. *Give me a fucking break*, he thought very often, spinning the chamber of his granddaddy's army-issue .45 and sometimes rubbing its long snout against his own, waiting for his chicken pot-pie to warm in the microwave, thinking, again and again, that this had to be the end of the line, that things simply could go no further, that . . .

When autumn arrived fallen leaves made the depressions in the yard plush and colorful. They collected in the pond and clotted, slowly soaking to an exquisite rot. Taftly observed this and believed he was going under as well. only not as beautifully.

For some reason, he was beginning to dwell on things that were far more cruel than anything he'd experienced. Suffering, his one loyal companion, had betrayed him at last. Now he constantly thought of fathers dying of cancer and leaving wives and children to fend for themselves, neglected old men in India lying atop piles of dead bodies, runaways forced into prostitution, snuff films, Dennis. The only ground left for Taftly to stand on was crumbling away like the leaves. It made him say, "Well, it *was* cruel what happened to you, Taftly, but you are a fucking ingrate for thinking so."

Such consideration simply left Taftly without a place in the world. He was supposed to be a loser, but if he wasn't really a loser by genuine loser standards, that meant he was a fraud or a parody of a loser, less than a loser, somehow, though, of course, not less than a loser in a way that had any integrity. Why, the more he thought of it, the more he realized he hadn't the right to even use the word. Loser was out-of-bounds, Taftly would have to settle for loner.

But that wasn't right, either. Loners were romantic sorts, possessed of a rough-hewn charm. Taftly had no business trying to tag himself a loner. Taftly, Taftly realized with a malicious snap of his fingers, did not deserve a full word. He merited a pre-word, perhaps, or maybe a mumble. At any rate, what was right for Taftly was some ugly sound that reached for word status but was denied it and yet remained so unspectacular in its failure that it would hardly be noticed.

Taftly attempted such a sound. *Ugh-mm.* This seemed promising if a little primal. *Uh-m.* There it was, barely, perfectly. Such a concoction, Taftly decided, could be categorized as an aborted chortle sprung from a tasteless remark. Taftly made the sound again. *Damn right,* he thought, slamming his palm down on the table—*I am an aborted chortle sprung from a tasteless remark.*

Nights weren't nearly so productive. Soon as the sun set, Taftly instigated gothic bouts of drinking. Once profoundly drunk, he routinely bolted from his house as if there were no longer enough room for him inside it. He hoped the end was near, yet he felt mired, going absolutely nowhere by way of a horribly circuitous route. The darkness before him seemed to be darkness incarnate and even the moonlight traded in darkness, drawing instead of giving light.

Standing barefoot on the cool night grass, Taftly would throw his head back in defiance. "Nietzsche was a romantic!" he'd bawl. Puffing on a clove, the taste of Fay deep into his nostrils and lungs—so near his heart—he'd continue to denounce the syphilitic philosopher until hoarse: "Nietzsche looked into the abyss and cringed! He couldn't endure it and started a fairy tale about willing power! Like anyone should give a shit! When God died it left a vacuum! It sucks! It's God's revenge! We are alone!"

Besotted with booze and passion, Taftly would eventually run down to the pond to lap water up from the surface of reflected stars like a crazed celestial dog while night after night, concealed behind a crepe myrtle, Dennis Jolly stretched the microphone to his new tape recorder as far as it would go in Taftly's direction.

X

THEN THERE WERE RUMORS FAY WAS PREGNANT. That
is how Taftly thought of them, as rumors, the same kind of
squalid accusations Rodney Train had thrown around. The
fact that Taftly had learned of Fay's pregnancy from Charlie,
and that Charlie had learned of Fay's pregnancy from Fay, did
not deter Taftly from insisting the information was tainted.

The first time Charlie told Taftly, something jagged
uncorked in Taftly's noggin, tearing past his eyes and bringing
his lids down. It hurt tremendously. Taftly swatted at his own
head to stop the pain. He felt dizzy and the floor seemed to
wantonly call up to him, inviting a dreadful copulation.

After walking unsteadily into the bathroom, he locked himself in a stall and vented frank tears, beating his fists against
horrid graffiti and bad language as his teeth sent out signals of
distress. When he could cry no more, he washed his face and
returned to his seat as if nothing had happened. His intention
was to appear very jaded, but he had the countenance of a

twelve-year-old working up the fortitude to order a Shirley Temple on the rocks.

"So that's the rumor," Taftly remarked.

"Rumor? Ain't no rumor. I got it straight from Fayceile. She's having a baby girl," Charlie explained.

"So they say," Taftly murmured.

"You know she'll be cute as a button. That Fay was always my favorite."

Charlie began polishing a glass, taking care of all the water spots with satisfaction. A few strands of hair had sprung from his ponytail and gathered about his chin but he didn't mind them.

"I guess there is a good Lord, after all," he continued. "Cause somebody sure was lookin after Fay." Hearty cigarette laughter caught in his throat and coughed out thickly. "That was the goddamndest thing in the world you did though. Ole Taftly Harper. You put a severe ass whipping on that fucking Train, boy. *De-railed* the sombitch! God damned amen to that! You took that one from a page out of your granddaddy's book. He would've been right proud."

Charlie looked at Taftly cheerfully, ready to offer him a drink, but when he saw Taftly's face he grew quiet and placed the rag on the counter.

"You been crying?" he whispered.

"No. I gouged my eye."

"Both of 'em, looks like," Oswald volunteered from down the way.

Charlie glared at him. "I want any shit outta you, Oswald, I'll pinch your damned head off, comprende?"

Taftly chugged several tea glasses of bourbon and headed to Fay's house that very evening. He'd made the trip many times before, usually when he was in no condition to drive. Pale, desperate and in need of a hopped-up blood transfusion, he'd crawl into his mother's fabulous Plymouth Fury and speed over to the town Fay inhabited, a pleasant hamlet a mere fifteen miles away.

The first time he saw Fay she was out on her front porch wearing over-alls, a striped engineer's cap such as brake-men once wore and very little else. Taftly saw the potential of such a get-up immediately—Fay could have been stripped bare with one swipe. She looked far from wifely, so beautiful it took Taftly's breath away. The second and third time it was the same. It would always be the same and Taftly was learning it the hard way.

Matters were not helped by the fact that the doctor had provided for Fay in precisely the manner Taftly believed she so richly deserved. It tormented him to see Fay skipping about such a resplendent domain. Every time Taftly thought of the place, he accused the doctor of trying to validate their unjustifiable union with mere trappings.

The night Taftly heard the vicious pregnancy rumor he stared at the white two-story antebellum manse and snorted, as was his custom. But with a baby on the way, Taftly resented the doctor extra. If will were power, he'd have sprouted horns and razed the entire edifice. He began examining the property for flaws, hoping to find evidence of something narrow-minded and supercilious like the doctor. Instead, he saw Fay.

She was tending a flower bed with a coal minor's lamp strapped to her head. It was magnificent. She worked her spade with a gentle quickness, sending merry glints in all directions, an angel looking after some forgotten chore. Taftly believed this was the single most delightful thing he'd ever seen done—Fay picking about the earth's crust after midnight with a beam of yellow light issuing from her forehead.

What, for the love of God, had driven her to such delectable weirdness? Was she, like Taftly, an insomniac and a tad kooky to boot? Did this tidy plot beckon to her each evening because she couldn't get Taftly out of her mind? Might they become agrarians together? Read and write poetry, make home-made wine and moonshine, tend fruitful crops, toil over goat-cheese recipes and make love through the night to the lowing of their curly-headed cattle? Did she miss him? Well, *did* she?

Taftly reached underneath the seat and fetched a pint of rein-forcement. Though Fay wasn't showing yet that he could tell, he knew in his heart it was true. Tucked away in his woodland hideout with Dennis, Taftly had become convinced that every-one was entrenched in the same old circumstances, perennially frozen in predicaments of pleasure or pain, but frozen nonethe-less. With Fay pregnant, however, he saw that the world had been clipping down the tracks toward a great destiny, leaving him far behind.

A swell of tears framed his vision just then. Fay was even more beautiful like that, swathed in a watery, heartfelt prism. Her edges fluttered and breathed cool light. It was clear to Taftly that she was going away. In the back of his mind, he'd always harbored feint hopes of a divorce for her and the doctor, but now he saw that wasn't going to happen.

A sudden blistering surge of tenderness tore from his chest, taking in Fay, the house and the unborn child at once. Why couldn't the little chap be Taftly's chap, Taftly wondered? And if the chap could not be Taftly's, why couldn't he, Taftly, love the chap anyway? Because Taftly believed he could, whether the chap was his or not. Not even a doctor's daughter could drive Taftly away from Fay—not even Fay could, who was, now that Taftly thought of it, a doctor's daughter as well. He would have them, the two doctor's daughters. All that was required was a death. The doctor's death. Or at least the doctor's disappearance. Either way, he liked the sound of it.

At some point in Taftly's reveries he elbowed the switch to the windshield wipers. They began shrieking, but Taftly was transfixed by thoughts of the doctor somehow choking on his own stethoscope or mistakenly prescribing himself a dose of hemlock instead of the stupid pills Taftly was sure the doctor popped by the dozen. Another thing Taftly didn't notice was a series of wild flashes coming from a window on the second-floor of the doctor's home. The action there was blinkering and heated, as if a mad scientist were straining to give birth to a new universe by spewing infant stars.

While Taftly kept to Fay, watching her with the kind of forlorn hunger experienced by a condemned man being served a final meal, the doctor began to pack up his camera. "Damned pervert," he hissed. This was the third time he'd spotted the Fury late at night. He'd wanted to tell Fay awhile ago but feared it would rattle her womb. Keeping Fay healthy and sound was the doctor's priority. It had become especially important lately because he wasn't feeling all that well. His migraines had returned and his appetite had vanished. He felt brittle. A colleague had recommended a check-up, but the doctor believed anything like that might upset the delicate balance he'd worked so hard to achieve. Everything had to remain the same until the baby came. All of which made him desperate to create an environment of perfect safety for his new family, something that did not include a Peeping Tom in a Fury.

The doctor lingered by the window growing furious. Though the salesman at the camera store told him he didn't have much chance shooting into the far darkness, the doctor had purchased a special camera with a telescopic lens and a gargantuan flash bulb anyway. He wanted to go to the police, but first he wanted evidence. That was what they'd taught him in medical school—to be meticulous and to consider things carefully. After all, it was entirely possible that the driver of the Fury was spying on his neighbor's daughter, a sixteen-year-old vixen who spent a lot of time in front of her bedroom window trying on different colored bras. Which reminded the doctor—was it really necessary for Fay to traipse about in the near nude while weeding at two in the morning?

When he'd first married her, he'd been extremely fond of her keen sensuality. He noticed, with pleasure, that everything she did dripped with significance and suggestion. She wasn't a flirt—sometimes sex seemed to be the farthest thing from her mind—but her way of moving and being was a continuous reproach to practicality, to artlessness, to just getting around and taking in air. He'd once seen her clipping her nails with a torpid determination that struck him as salacious, her tongue lingering up around her teeth, searching, probing . . .

Those damned teeth. I want her to take them out for me, he thought suddenly. *No, Christ, I don't! I didn't think that! I didn't!*

His temples began to throb then and the veins webbing his head and neck twitched peevishly, undulations which brought to mind the hideous dance-work accomplished by the seething ganglia of a man-o-war. A migraine was in striking distance. The doctor became perfectly still, as if to hide from it, but it was too late and he knew it. The migraine had caught him thinking something dirty about his wife and he was going to pay for it.

"Go home you bastard! Go home! Get off my street!" He winced and held up his hand as if to fend off a blow. "I want everything clean! Why can't it be clean? Everything right where it belongs! Nothing like *that!* No past! No past! Oh, god it hurts!"

Taftly heard the shouts but could not be sure where they came from. When Fay walked back in the house, he noticed his wipers and felt foolish and a little sober. He shut them off and drove away, promising, as he did each time he visited, that he would never return again.

A slight pang of respect for the doctor closed Taftly's mouth as he left the town limits. The doctor had done nothing wrong other than going bald and flabby. Taftly knew him to be a supremely decent being, in fact. He'd heard that he went to Honduras each year to volunteer medical services. He sang in the choir and earned wild sums of money from cutting people open, something he was quite good at.

Taftly banged the steering wheel to emphasize the doctor's goodness. Really, Taftly, Taftly thought, why can't you leave the happy couple alone? What sort of seed do you think you have anyway? After the rough handling you took in that field, you ought to consider castration. There's no family for you with anyone you'd care to have and you are one of those especially disgusting people who are disgusted with the kind of people you deserve. Which meant, Taftly suddenly realized, that he didn't even deserve the sort of people he deserved.

"The Clydesdales did you a favor!" he cried. He punched the accelerator and growled. "It was *pity* they showed you!"

Around the bend a Starvin Marvin convenience store glowed freakishly in the night like an enormous slot machine set down in the woods. It called Taftly in warmly, yet under the fierce lights of the parking lot he was further embarrassed by the cycle of hope, contempt, regret and finally shame that accompanied every trip to Fay's neighborhood. His teeth seemed to shift and twist within their gummy homes and Taftly got the idea that they were pleased to see him suffer.

Brian, the kid who worked the night shift at the Starvin Marvin, waved to Taftly. Although seemingly brainless, the youngster had been extremely kind to him from the very first journey. He had tanning-bed skin and a soft voice. His hair had been bleached until the strands appeared pasted onto his head. He smiled a lot. When Taftly walked inside, he spotted him a peace sign. "What's up, dude?"

Taftly fingered a modest return and nodded. "Not much." He walked over to the soda fountain and filled a jumbo cup with ice and a touch of coke. "Keeping everything under control tonight?"

"Sure. Hey, guess what, man? My girlfriend and I broke up."

"I'm sorry."

"Oh, no. It didn't last long. She came in here tonight and we talked it out. So I think we're back together. I guess. I don't know. I'm probably going to wait for at least an hour before calling her again, you know, just to play it loose."

Taftly lingered by the magazine rack. There was another shot of a female runner nearly galloping off the page. A bead of perspiration filled the sweet cleft above her lip and Taftly almost reached for it.

"I don't mean to get personal or anything but I was just wondering—do you come over here for a girl or something?" Brian asked.

"Not really."

Taftly cupped his hand as if to give the runner a place to go. He imagined her treading up his arm and assuming life size proportions about his neck, perched there like a trophy.

"I was going to say, 'cause, like, dude, all the good-looking women in this town are either my age or married."

Taftly looked up. "*Your* age. How old do you think I am?"

Brian shrugged politely. "Thirty or something."

"Is that old?"

"Older than high school, dude."

Taftly sat in the Fury and mixed a drink. He checked the rear-view mirror to see how old he looked. It was too dark to tell for sure, but Taftly believed that his recent tortures had aged him. In fact, the more he examined himself, the more he believed they'd been fashioned to fit the fault-lines of his nature and to dig and bury themselves there until there were wrinkles and scars. All the blond hairs on his arms were turning dark and the dark hairs on his head were being spoiled by resolute strands of grey which were course and horsey. His face had grown longer and more serious. His lips were somehow smaller and always tightly set. Taftly found them bloodless and a touch sinister and could not imagine a woman wanting to kiss them. He occasionally pinched them to make them pay for going bad on him. Worse still, his toes groped out awkwardly as if they were odds and ends hastily collected from some discount charnel house. As a child, they'd curled down in sleek harmony. Where had his good toes run off to?

Taftly took a courageous swig, saluted the clerk and drove into the night. The runner could not keep up with him and soon he was alone again. With the windows down, the air smelled of pine and oak and heavily of the loam of dusty leaves and rich eartht. Where there were breaks in the trees a bracing aroma of grass and fertilized soil wafted across the highway, which looked freshly spilt and precarious in the moonlight. Taftly motored on, hungry for his lane to culminate in some doomed precipice that he would traverse with bravery, his hands freed from the wheel at last.

Hunkered down into his seat, he began warmly spelling out the details of this last ride when he caught sight of Dennis walking down the highway. He tried to pretend he hadn't seen Dennis, but Dennis prevented this by jumping in front of the Fury. Taftly swerved onto the shoulder to avoid striking him down. As soon as he realized he'd steered clear of Dennis he regretted it.

"What the hell are you doing?" Taftly demanded.

"I reckon I could ask the same of you," Dennis replied.

"I guess you want a ride."

"No way, Jose. I'm just getting started. Tonight's the night. I've done calculations." He tapped a contented beat on his fanny pack and grinned.

"For what?" Taftly asked, instantly incensed with himself for having fallen into another of Dennis's conversational snares.

"For abductions. Look up there. If this ain't the right night I don't know what is."

Taftly wanted Dennis to be abducted. He wondered if there were anything he could do to ensure it. "What do you think your chances are?" he asked.

"Fifty-fifty," Dennis announced.

Taftly was considering this, wishing the odds were better, when he heard a loony barking noise. It was coming from Dennis's portable cassette player, from the earphones which hung around Dennis's neck.

"What are you listening to?" Taftly asked.

"Wouldn't you like to know?" Dennis crowed.

"Yes. I would. That's why I'm asking."

"Sure. I bet."

"Forget it."

"This here's a lecture, partner," Dennis said, stopping the tape. "Don't get yer g-strang in a wad." He smiled a smile that made Taftly want to punish his face with a flat-head shovel.

"A lecture? What kind of lecture?"

"A pretty damned good one, old buddy. I've got a whole series of 'em, matter of fact. I'm thinking on marketing 'em. They'd fetch a fair price from the students up at the college, I reckon. Put a little ad in the paper and what not. I figure the aliens wouldn't mind having a gander neither. This is the sort of stuff that'd freak them right out of their space contraption. They don't know everything, trust me on that one."

"By who?"

"What?"

"The lecture."

"By whom," Dennis corrected. Next he acted as if he were bored. "Listen, I've got to keep going if there's any chance at all of contact. You're just the type to scare 'em away."

This made perfect sense to Taftly. He put the Fury in gear.

"Oh, by the way, I thought you didn't like the aliens. I thought they humiliated you, made you crap your pants and such."

Dennis drew back from the window. He fiddled with his cap and sighed, then looked down the highway somberly, sighting something with his thumb. "Yeah, but the thing is, it gets in your blood sometimes," he explained.

XI

EARLY THE NEXT MORNING, Taftly spotted Dennis poking about the shore line with a long aluminum pole, puncturing the earth for no good reason. He'd probably been at it before dawn, Taftly estimated, getting a head-start on packing the day with wasted hours.

Taftly closed his curtains and walked into the kitchen. He prepared a large breakfast of creamed eggs, bacon and cheese grits to cool his hangover. He ate appreciatively, nodding as the pain slowly condensed into a small and manageable knot of fatigue just behind his eyes.

With that taken care of, he returned to the window and was flabbergasted. Dennis was still out there and had become more ludicrous. Having waded waist-deep into the pond, he was attempting to spear fish, jobbing at bluegill and curious bass, though not very effectively. He was also, Taftly noticed, engaged in a running commentary on his efforts, as if he were an exotic native being filmed for a documentary.

Without a cloud in sight, it was useless to hope for lightning. The aliens had failed once again and now Taftly would pay for it. The price would be especially high as Taftly had to go into town. Whenever Dennis caught Taftly on his way to one of the automobiles, he insisted on a lift. That meant a ten-minute ride which had the potential to take years off Taftly's life, or at the very least, tempt him to retrieve a screwdriver from the glove compartment and pierce his own ear drums.

For this reason Taftly was forced to peer from the windows of his cabin like a fugitive, waiting for Dennis to disappear into his shack, where, Taftly knew, he sometimes spent hours thumbing through the dog-eared pages of muscle magazines. There were female bodybuilders, Dennis had informed him, and Dennis thought most highly of them. When not actually pumping iron, they spent most of their time oiled-up and naked in front of the camera. That was Dennis's idea of how a woman ought to pass the time, buffed up in the buff, and he was forever recommending such behavior to any female hapless enough to find herself in conversation with him.

But the remarkable thing about Taftly's attempts to escape his own house was that no matter how crafty his efforts to get clear of Dennis he seldom succeeded, for in addition to the quality of superfluity, Dennis also exhibited an alarming and miraculous ubiquity. There was no way of knowing when Dennis would appear, only *would* appear, trailing misery and discontent behind him like a pair of noisy shackles.

Often, after hours of mousing from window to window,

Taftly would break from the front door, race to the car and rocket into town only to find Dennis sitting on a bench in front of the courthouse. As soon as Dennis spotted Taftly he'd begin flagging him down. The sight was appalling—Dennis's arms gesticulated like two breeding windmills being shat up by a category five hurricane. He did this sincerely, as if he and Taftly were long lost pals who had not seen one another in years.

"Hey, I got ya something," Dennis would call desperately.

Unless Taftly wanted Dennis to chase after him, he had to park his car and walk over. Horribly, Dennis always produced something from his fanny pack in broad daylight. He usually offered a newspaper article pertaining to a government agency gone amok or an advertisement for some new weight lifting supplement.

The dark secret of Taftly's life—aside from the Clydesdales and the fact that the woman of his dreams had removed her front teeth to service him—was that he and Dennis were in league together in order to build Taftly a better body. Here again was another untoward outcome of the Clydesdale debacle.

Taftly no longer wanted to be lean. He wanted, *needed,* to be formidable. His dream was to be able to seriously hurt people without giving it much thought. Too often he whiled away his time directing daydreams in which he was almost constantly bumping into fiends and accidently rupturing their spleens or dislocating their backs and never realizing it until amazed crowds gathered to inspect the carnage so carelessly piled behind him.

With Dennis's assiduous pursuit of weight training minutia, Taftly was getting there. Though thin, Dennis was ruthlessly strong and a student of the martial arts. Taftly was learning to defend himself with his hands and feet. They sparred out by the pond, sometimes getting angry and a little bloody toward sunset. During such sessions, Dennis became entranced and often feigned an Asian accent. This deeply humiliated Taftly, but then humiliation was Taftly's *forte* if not his *raison d'etre*.

Taftly had purchased several thousand dollars worth of equipment—benches, racks, barbells, dumbbells—all per Dennis's specific instructions. When they unloaded everything into the canning shed, Dennis began licking his lips and ordering the workmen around in a grievous falsetto that Taftly feared might be sexual. He was soon to learn there were more substantial things to worry about, however, for once the weight room had been set up, Dennis declared himself to be Taftly's trainer and donned a coach's whistle. He took the trainer designation very seriously, bandying it about town. This was easily the most loathsome aspect of the beefing up regimen, yet another hair-suit with matching barbed-wire boxers to add to Taftly's ever-expanding martyr's wardrobe.

A further problem was that Dennis, having anointed himself Taftly's personal trainer, assumed that he and Taftly had become confidantes. They were tight, two-of-a-kind, he and Taftly, loners who'd forsaken the world for the simple and difficult pleasures of country life. Dennis had pieced together three or four serviceable things to say about Nietzsche in order to cement the partnership, not realizing that Taftly despised the man. He found that Nietzsche aphorisms fit him perfectly. What is more, he began to roll his own, as he believed any respectable *Uberman* would.

"Life without music would be a mistake," he'd announce, his radio blasting a horrible variety of pop-country while he tapped tobacco into a heavily slavered paper. "Know what I mean?" If Taftly didn't respond, he'd shout the insight across the pond. "A damned mistake, Taft. Ya know?"

But Dennis's belief that he and Taftly were peas in a pod of existential angst was nothing compared to his conviction that he and Taftly had the same taste in women. "Smart but not too smart," Dennis would assert with a wink. "We ain't the type to settle for them big butts," he'd whisper, nodding cagily. "Nor over-the-top-heavy neither."

In such a spirit Dennis had once waved Taftly down on the square in order to show him an advertisement which struck Taftly as perhaps the most depraved thing he'd ever seen. It was an order form for videos. These videos, which Dennis began talking very loudly about, featured body-building women who wrestled and subdued weak men by way of various leg-locks about the face. Topless and saddled with thongs the width of dental floss, they were covered head-to-toe in baby oil. Taftly wanted to slap Dennis into a life-long coma, but instead snatched the advertisement away and told him to never again show him anything so vile.

"You're a little late," Dennis huffed.

"Late how?"

"I already ordered us up a couple of them tapes C.O.D. They'll be here next week."

"Shit."

"Shit nothing. You'll end up thanking me," Dennis retorted as Taftly stormed away. The rebuff stung and Dennis wanted relief. "He's uppity. Uppity-tight," he said sullenly.

On the morning Taftly stared out his front window watching Dennis pretend to spear fish—the morning after Dennis had not been abducted by the feckless aliens—Dennis accomplished an unprecedented violation. Up to his waist in cool water, plugging away with the long aluminum pole which he'd used for an antennae before his satellite dish came in, Dennis grew listless. He'd been hoping that Taftly would appear on the front porch and offer him a ride into town, but that hadn't happened and he decided to change pants and thumb a ride. He hadn't seen Rene in almost a week and couldn't wait any longer.

Dennis was in the habit of loitering about the Western Union counter at the washeteria, steadily driving the Western Union girl, Rene Tutwiler, toward permanent residence in the nut house by draping himself over the counter, flexing his sinewy muscles and calling her "Sweet Thing," which he pronounced "Sweet Thang."

"Sweet Thang, anybody wired me yet?"

"Who would send you anything?" Rene routinely queried. " 'Cept maybe a straight jacket."

"They don't have one that'd fit me," Dennis would crow, striking a pose that favored his triceps.

By the time Dennis made it into town he'd been helped down the highway by three unsuspecting drivers who could not believe their rotten luck. Dennis, on the other hand, was invigorated. As soon as he entered the washeteria he began lying.

"Caught me a fifteen pound bass this morning."

"Bullhockey," Rene said.

"Did so. Know what else?"

"Please leave."

"Speared the sombitch."

"What, with your breath?"

"Hee. Hee."

"How much would it cost me to get you to never come in here again?" Rene wanted to know.

"A kiss." Whereupon Dennis mustered some quick thinking and blurted a revision. "Open mouthed."

"Well, if you've got to come in here, at least quit talking," Rene replied.

Unfortunately for Rene, Dennis believed this was a form of feisty flirtation. He puckered and Rene retreated behind the counter, searching for the staple gun. She was thinking about tripping herself up and firing a stable into Dennis's thrapple. Dennis's thrapple made her squirm. She'd learned about thrapples from some book she'd read long ago. The thrapple was the nexus of the throat and Adam's apple—the thrapple—that much she remembered. Dennis needed a staple through his. It would shut him up and make him a better person. Rene was imagining this when she remembered the telegram.

"Hey, Dennis, don't you live out there at Taftly Harper's new place?"

"Somewhat, Sweet Thang. Would you care to see the grounds?"

"If I die first. Any-who, Taftly's got a telegram. I've been calling him for three days now, but he don't answer. We never get telegrams anymore. It's mostly people wiring money." Rene pursed her lips. "Matter of fact, this is the first telegram I've ever seen. How quaint."

"Telegram? From who?"

"From whom," she corrected. "And that's none of your business, Nosey Parker."

Unconvinced of Dennis's repeated assertions of martial arts prowess, she held up the telegram enticingly, whereupon Dennis karate chopped it from her hand. He emitted a sound which he believed faithfully reproduced a samurai's manly war cry, but instead brought to mind a pierced balloon flatulently careening across a sound chamber.

"Give that back this instant," Rene squalled.

"I'll take it to him myself. I'm his personal trainer. Hell, he'd be nothing but dead without me," Dennis insisted.

"Give it back. I mean it. Give it."

Dennis smiled, blew Rene a kiss, re-holstered an imaginary six shooter with a quick thrust of the hips and spun toward the door. Once on the street, he unzipped his fanny pack and tucked the telegram inside it.

Later that afternoon, safely within his deluxe shack, Dennis tried a trick he'd learned on TV. He struck a match and held the envelope above the flame to read its contents.

Taftly Harper.

Dennis stopped reading and said "Stop." It made him giggle. He tried to read the next line but was so tickled with himself he began cooing like a pigeon. "Stop!" he cried. "Stop! Stop!" Sometimes he was just too much, he thought. "You really crack me up!" he said to himself. Then he noticed the smoke. He looked into his lap, howled and pitched the envelope across the room.

"Damnit to hell!" he wailed, wringing his burnt finger in the air.

He blamed Taftly and cursed him. Next he reviled Western Union for being so irresponsible as to not fire-proof their envelopes. He promised to file a lawsuit. "We'll just see where the dadblamed profit motive gets ya! Bastards!"

It then occurred to Dennis that the telegram lay shrinking and browning on the kitchen floor. He rushed to stomp the flames and fell to his knees. "Dear God! Please heal the telegram!" he prayed.

A few clean inches were left in the top right-hand corner. With the wedge held up to the light, he saw that the message had gone up in smoke. It was not much of a healing and already Dennis feared God and Taftly's coming wrath. He quickly put on his thinking cap, an accessory held in reserve for just such emergencies. He placed it lightly atop his baseball cap, just so, and patted it before closing his eyes.

His opinion was this: Do unto others as you would have them do unto you.

Dennis liked the Golden Rule. It was his favorite. "It's golden," he frequently pointed out. He mouthed the rule quite a lot in front of Taftly, as a matter of fact, which had the effect of convincing Taftly that whatever the doctrine of the incarnation meant, it could not have meant that Christ was aware of all future states, else how could Christ have possibly let loose with such a maxim knowing Dennis was only a few thousand years down the pike. No one in their right mind would want to be treated the way Dennis wanted to be treated.

After studying the charred document, Dennis applied the Golden Rule to it. He, for one, wouldn't want a telegram that had been burnt up and couldn't be read. That was just the kind of thing to annoy Dennis Jolly. That would be *unconscionable*.

Dennis made a face which he believed comported with carrying out his duty. It was a face he'd seen on late-night movies when brave men were being tortured or had to walk the gangplank after pirates had taken over a ship. Braced like this, he went to the commode and flushed the remains.

He felt badly about having to do it, but cheered himself by

contemplating his latest scheme: He was going to make Taftly famous. Any day, his high-speed cassette duplicator would arrive. It had cost an entire government check but would it ever be worth it. As soon as he had the ability to dupe Taftly's nightly discourses, he would be in business. "Taftly'll thank me then," he allowed. He grew teary thinking about it.

Crouched behind the crepe myrtle night after night, holding out the microphone, Dennis often imagined giving lectures about Taftly once he'd established Taftly's reputation as a deranged genius. He believed honorary degrees and adoring coeds would follow. Out of deep gratitude, Taftly would invite Dennis to live next door to him in a sister mansion. They'd telephone each other throughout the day to discuss important topics. After securing wives and children, they'd home school.

"Taftly's the only true friend I've ever had," Dennis stated softly. "He's the only one that takes me seriously." He smiled, dropping a tear. "He even gets mad at me. Nobody else does. Nobody else thinks I count enough to be mad at. Not Taftly."

But lately, Dennis reflected, Taftly's lectures had become deflated. His rage was fleeting. He didn't battle the great philosophers much any more. Truth be told, Taftly hadn't actually done anything but sniffle for weeks, strolling around the pond with a heedlessness that remarked not confidence but some creeping development of invisibility. Taftly seemed so completely disappeared, in fact, that sometimes Dennis rubbed his eyes to be certain he had not been taken in by an optical illusion. *Could be something along the lines of his astral body projecting out there*, Dennis once caught himself thinking.

Dennis was worried. What was more clear to him than ever broke his heart, and he knew he would not get better than twelve hours sleep a night until he'd done something about it—Taftly believed God had forgotten him. But God hadn't forgotten him, not one bit, not with Dennis Jolly on the case.

Dennis saw the entire predicament as his own personal trial. His task was to be patient and serve as an example to Taftly. And it would take patience, to be sure, because Taftly, in Dennis's opinion, had had all the advantages. He had money and a fancy granddaddy. Women didn't run away from him. He sported about in dapper clothes, even when alone in the cabin. Speaking of which, he had one. When he quit his job driving the water truck and Dennis had asked how he'd make ends meet, Taftly huffed that he'd just have to keep trading up in the stock market. Furthermore, Taftly owned a nice stereo and could keep his mouth shut when he wanted to.

Still, Dennis felt sorry for Taftly. He believed God had made Taftly for the express purpose of allowing Dennis to show him how exceptional he was. The day Taftly moved in Dennis knew that he would probably have to teach Taftly something important. Perhaps that was why Dennis had been made poor and broken down, to reach Taftly. Perhaps all of Taftly's life had been awaiting the day he would meet Dennis Jolly and be brought right to God, which meant, Dennis realized, that all of *his* life, or at least a worthy part of it, had been a preparation for meeting Taftly.

Ya got to keep sharp though, Dennis reminded himself. *Got to quit talking 'bout them damned aliens.* He felt ashamed for pretending to be pitiful and crazy now that there was work to do.

Dennis peered across the pond at Taftly's cabin. The sun was setting over it. Dennis thought the sun looked like a fat round egg cooked sunny side up with rich orange rivulets running across the darkening plate of the sky. He believed it symbolized a promise of some sort. "Good morning," he said, his chest thumping with determination in the golden twilight. He had really not amounted to very much over the course of his life, he admitted, but it seemed that things might change at last.

Taftly came out then, sockless. Though slung low in threadbare khakis, a sagely wrinkled hundred dollar oxford and Jack Purcell tennis shoes, his cultivated disregard was demolished by the fact that he ran to his car as if trying to escape being stoned.

Dennis shook his head, every inch of him the wizened and indulgent father. "God bless him, but that boy acts plum nutty sometimes."

XII

Taftly did not slow down until he saw the steeple. Then the rest emerged, ponderous and overbearing, like a massive ship landed on a tiny island, floodlights shining up everything—corners, doorways, sidewalks, flower beds—while ticking halogen globes towered along the perimeter of the parking lot, showering a surreal clarity over each cleanly outlined space. Taftly took one and waited.

The stolid bricks of the sanctuary, administration offices, day-care facility, youth center, K-6 academy, and gymnasium occupied an entire block, marking out a squat reddish territory of righteousness and felled trees. This last bothered Taftly, and he rifled himself for fond memories of the old church with its stately arbor of cedars, beneath which he and Sunday school chums would ferret out stones to throw at one another while inside the elders were praying.

Sick with sin, the children threw stones simply to hurt one another. That's what gave them pleasure. But he recalled cures—vacation bible school in the summer and snow cones. He'd once memorized the entire thirteenth chapter of First Corinthians for a double scoop with all five flavors, a suicide that signalled he was well on his way to learning that the hellish little minions who accompanied him to the playgrounds, backyards, woods and fields with all manner of evil on their minds were actually created in the image of God. Taftly knew this had to be a miracle even then.

How he wished for a cigarette. He looked around for something else to absorb and came again to the steeple. It seemed sadly marooned in utilitarian excess and Taftly's spirit went up to it, trying to rise with it and be happy. This was his second trip into town without Dennis in a single day and he was feeling he should feel fortunate.

After a few minutes Pastor Bates came waddling out. He pumped Taftly's hand, his left eye narrowing with excitement. "How 'bout the Catfish Cabin?"

Taftly shrugged. "I guess you want to drive."

Pastor Bates took in the olive Fury with a dismissive sputter. "You got that right."

There was a praise tape playing in Pastor Bates's black Lincoln Town Car. Taftly leaned into the chilly leather, inhaling its aroma. He almost began clapping out a beat. The Lincoln was like a big thunder cloud of pleasure floating down the road with its own choir in tow.

"You remember that old preacher your mama used to carry you off to every now and again?"

"Brother Streeter?"

"Brother T.C. Streeter, indeed. He died the other day. I went out to his funeral. Weird old coot, but he was the real deal. A hundred years old. They say he asked God if he could please die. And you know how it was with him and God. God didn't deny T.C. Streeter much."

Taftly remembered Brother Streeter well. He had possessed the gift of knowledge and offered stunningly accurate visions, which he rendered with an almost artistic care, something Taftly learned at a very young age. When Taftly had one day come home from school touting Camus, his mother, to his enormous disappointment, hadn't really argued about it. "After all God's done for us?" is all she said.

"He's damn near ruined us, mama," Taftly snapped.

"What did you say?" She stared him down, tapping her shoe the while. "You come with me young man. We're just going to have to see Brother Streeter."

The backwoods prophet greatly troubled Taftly. What if he produced some revelation in front of Taftly's mother? Taftly had just then entered puberty and the idea of anyone reading his mind terrified him.

"Okay! I believe! I believe!" Taftly pleaded.

"No siree. You're an atheist," his mother insisted

The trip required them to drive an hour away to the out-skirts of a settlement known as Claw Junction, pop. 23. His mother, though already thirty pounds beyond her prime in those days, could still look attractive in a disturbingly provocative way when she wore church clothes and gussied up with lip stick. She was like an over-ripe piece of fruit which had a few days left before rottenness set in, the kind of a woman that men developed vast cravings for when drunk. Taftly sensed all of this, and it made the journey to Brother Streeter's even more horrendous. Everything—the car, the trees, the sky— became sticky and melted into a florid ooze that hummed along with Taftly's pulse.

Worse, as soon as the old man saw Taftly he smiled craftily, as if he were presently to reveal a secret about masturbation and put Taftly on his heels for good.

"Tell him, Taftly," Taftly's mother shrieked.

Taftly shuffled about in the expectant silence until his mother took his wrist and gave it a quick jerk.

"Sir," Taftly began, avoiding Brother Streeter's eyes. "I'm thinking on becoming an atheist."

Brother Streeter muted his grin and asked Taftly's mother to leave the room. After the door shut, he offered Taftly a seat in a folding chair. For a few delicate moments, he fingered the crease in his trousers with quiet dignity. Taftly noticed this—it seemed important, the practice of some lost art.

"You ought not to blame girl troubles on God," the old man said finally. His voice was roomy and irresistible. It reminded Taftly of the attenuated pull of gravity when bouncing on a trampoline. "What if God answered your prayers? What if he made all them girls want you? Would they *really* want you? That's the predicament."

"Hey, how'd you know about the girl part?" Taftly asked, astounded at the facility with which Brother Streeter had cut to the chase. He had only felt like a stranger in the world—unknown to himself or anyone other than Camus—after having been turned down twice for the school dance. "Is that the gift? The gift of knowledge?"

"No, son. That's being old. Common sense."

"Do the gift on me!" Taftly blurted. Perhaps God would reveal a girl who would accompany him to the dance, preferably one who was already developing nicely.

"*Do the gift on you?*" Brother Streeter roared. "Listen, I ain't no Ouija board. This ain't magic. I'd have to seek God's face about you, come before the Lord on your behalf. Slippery as you are, it could take months. Might even have to fast."

"You mean you ain't never sought God on my behalf before?"

"Son, no offense, but I cain't say that you've ever once crossed my mind."

Taftly was sure he would cry. The man was a genuine prophet and did not even know Taftly existed.

"Will you try to think of me sometime," Taftly requested meekly.

"Tell ya what, from now on, yer on the list," Brother Streeter allowed. He dabbed some anointing oil onto his thumb and touched Taftly's forehead then. His prayer began as a whisper but quickly grew intense. Suddenly, he looked up as if he'd been startled, straining at Taftly, his pupils black pinpoints of shock.

"What?" Taftly said.

"You're very prominently on God's mind," the old man said, incredulous.

"*Me?*"

"I know. It's puzzling."

As soon as they walked into the Catfish Cabin Taftly spotted the corner booth where he and Fay had spoken of love, the very booth where they'd sat side-by-side like a couple direct from France. The waitress took them to another booth at Taftly's request, but Taftly felt lost in it and his eyes kept drifting back to the corner that had once held such promise. He wondered what Fay was doing and recalled her wonderful table manners. Though she'd been reared elegantly, Taftly figured her teeth probably added to her discrete charm. He blushed, remembering the tiny bites of catfish she'd taken and her gentle cheerful chewing.

"You said you had something important to talk to me about," Taftly said, trying to forget his last meal with Fay.

Pastor Bates smiled without pleasure and tapped the table. When he finished tapping, he finished smiling. "Yeah. I do." He sighed. "It's about your father."

Taftly jerked back, his face stunned and blameless.

"I've been meaning to talk to you about this for some time now," Pastor Bates continued.

Taftly remembered being at the Catfish Cabin long ago,

after closing time, when his granddaddy and his daddy had argued. Most of the lights were out and the owner, Inez, had sent the staff home, or so Taftly supposed, as he was certain the place had been empty save for them. An oil lamp burned brightly on their table and Taftly watched his granddaddy turn it down, wincing as he did so, then rubbing his fingers, taking Taftly in with concern and frustration. Curiously, Taftly couldn't recall where his mother had been that night. Perhaps she'd been at church, or perhaps she'd simply gone to bed and since Taftly often had trouble sleeping his father had been forced to carry Taftly along to the late supper. They'd brought in a fifth of bourbon, Taftly was sure of that. It was an easy mark for the memory of a five-year-old, especially since his granddaddy had taught him about quarts, pints, fifths and gallons with bottles of booze. A fifth was tall and sleek and momentous. Taftly could see Taftly watching his granddaddy pour from it.

Once they were well into the whisky and sated with catfish, Taftly's granddaddy became irritated and voluble. *You have a responsibility now!* he charged. And he almost did, as if leading a cavalry—almost charged right in front of his words as if to dispel any suspicion of cowardice, as if to be certain the words would fight and keep fighting. Yet Taftly's daddy held his ground: *I'll be back,* he said softly. He smiled at Taftly. Taftly asked his daddy where he was going and could he join him. *Inez, please come take Taftly out back to show him the catfish pond,* his granddaddy called as his long fingers curled around the bottle impatiently. Inez hurried over. *Come on*, she said, taking Taftly's wrist. But Taftly didn't want to go and tried to twist free. If he was going to cry he did not want to do it on the run. Then his granddaddy was talking again: *No, damnit, you won't be back. You think you will but you won't.* When Inez found better purchase, Taftly went stiff. Making himself rigid as a miniature cadaver, the toes of his patent-leather buckle-my-shoes pointed up as his heels slid across the floor. He closed his eyes until a cool lick of a breeze parted his silken blond hair, then stared hard the bald face of the night sky. *Where's daddy going?* But no answer was given and years later he knew none ever would be.

Taftly looked up. Pastor Bates had arranged a game of checkers on the checkered table cloth, pink packets of imitation sugar versus white packets of pure bleached cane. After jumping three imitations, Pastor Bates lifted his eyes. His hands went to his sides and remained as if tethered to his hips.

"Maybe we should wait until we get back to my study," he said.

XIII

PASTOR BATES CULLED A CLUSTER OF KEYS from his trouser pocket, jangling out lint and the powdery remains of a crushed breath mint before pinching the proper key between his index finger and thumb. He motioned and Taftly followed down the dark hallway, their steps illuminated by the ruby distillation of an emergency exit sign.

Though Taftly had always considered empty sanctuaries the perfect place to rest anxious bones, on this night the atmosphere seemed *noire* and not a little creepy. Furthermore, at some point during the drive into town his teeth had become plump as ticks, yet fragile. It seemed as if they were unfinished. He thought of them as plaster creations that hadn't dried or hardened. Should he nick or grind one, he sensed it would break away or be bent into an odd or useless shape, and he held his mouth still to prevent this.

"Come on in," Pastor Bates said.

The study was crammed floor to ceiling with books. Aside

from a few sappy and second-rate devotional and counseling texts, almost all of them were good. Pastor Bates was a careful reader of theology, literature and history. He delighted especially in Gibbon's woeful treatment of Christians in *The Decline and Fall of the Roman Empire,* perusing the fifteenth and sixteenth chapters routinely and with glee. He enjoyed brilliant heretics as only the confidently faithful can, seeing in Gibbon the inspired rantings of a cheerleader working himself into a frenzy for a losing team, getting especially rabid come the dreaded fourth quarter when Jesus begins running up the score. Whereas Taftly wanted to kick Nietzsche, Pastor Bates got a kick *out of* Nietzsche. "Imagine a man being so grandiose as to mistake his own loss of faith for the death of God," he'd once remarked.

Taftly read titles and minded his teeth. Pastor Bates waited. A minute passed and Taftly switched to another case. It could have gone that way for the rest of the night, Pastor Bates surmised, and so he began. "There's a lot you don't know about your mama and daddy," he stated.

Taftly brought his eyes over slowly. He'd somehow managed to recapture a petulant arrogance lost to him since his teens. "Oh, I'm sure," he said. He kissed his thumb tips and began to twiddle.

"There's some things I think you should know is all."

"I know he left us. I know he never came back for granddaddy's funeral. Or mother's. He never tried to contact us. That's what I know. He may as well be dead. That's how I think of him, in fact—as dead. He might even be dead for all I know."

"Well, actually . . ." Pastor Bates swiveled in his chair, searching for a better angle. He felt it might ease the situation should he utter something profound from a state of repose, but the desired perch eluded him and the chair tipped back with an obscene whinny. "That happens to not be true, for one thing," he said after regaining his balance.

"You mean he's not dead," Taftly quipped, still reading titles.

Pastor Bates frowned. "Your father *did* try to contact you, as a matter of fact. Several times. I suspect you know that. Your mother wouldn't allow it."

Taftly was shaking his head.

"That's not all. He learned of your granddaddy's death too late to make the funeral, but he came in town for your mama's funeral. He didn't go out there to the grave site, he had his reasons, good or bad, but he was right here in Copiah Springs."

"Where?"

"He stayed with me. Sat right in my house and waited for me to come back and tell him it was over. He stayed in town two more days looking for you. You never showed up at the house. Didn't show up in town, either. We never did find out where you'd gone."

"I was with some friends." A bilious secretion filled Taftly's chest. He wondered if it would be possible to spew it across

Pastor Bates's desk and burn up his sermon notes. "So, y'all are big buddies I guess," he hissed.

"Your daddy has handled things the way he wanted to. I haven't often agreed with him and more than once I've tried to change his mind but he'd never budge. It's complicated. You can either go through life tinkering or taking the long view. My job is to take the long view, to keep trying. I certainly don't expect you to like any of this. I sure wouldn't. And besides, there's so much you don't know. You don't even really know how they got together do you?"

Taftly did not know, as a matter of fact. He'd never given the subject much consideration. From conversations with his mother he'd assumed his daddy had simply abused his way into the marriage. His thoughts about their courtship had always been severely Russian, brooding images of his mother, impoverished, vulnerable, succulent, being hounded and overrun by his daddy, impudent and aristocratic, a horse-beater and a rougher-upper of women, especially virgins.

"They were in love," Pastor Bates was saying. He thought about this. "Well, somewhat. Your daddy was in college, it was about his second or third year, I guess. I was in law school then. We became friends. Your mama was still in high school. What a beauty. Your daddy was crazy about her but he wasn't ready to get married. He'd always wanted to travel. Wanted to spend a few years just shuffling around, then he planned on coming back home. He wanted to run the bank, be a banker. Isn't that something?"

"A banker."

"Then your mother got pregnant."

Taftly's eyes fired. "Isn't that something."

"Anyhow, after you were about five or six he decided he could afford to take off for a month or two. It was a crazy idea, I know, but he did it and it turned out he was gone much longer, but that wasn't entirely his fault. By the time he tried to come back, your mother wanted no part of it. She asked him to stay away. Demanded it, really. She'd come to hate him. Which I don't blame her."

"Which I don't either."

"She needed to be fought for at that point. She wanted him to *insist* on their marriage, to force the issue. A woman gets to that point sometimes. But your daddy just took her at her word and left town again. Hurt her so badly that she wouldn't take any Harper money from that day on. That's when that started. Moved y'all out of that big house your granddaddy had given as a wedding present. Burned all her dresses. That was a bad time."

Pastor Bates crunched his mouth sullenly.

"I'll tell you one thing," he said, holding up a pencil. "It liked to've killed your granddaddy. You were the apple of his eye, and every time he tried to spend a dime on you your mother threw whatever he'd bought away. Only thing she ever let him help with was that piano, and I guess that was because she wanted you to play so bad. She always used to ask me if you could play at the church once you got good enough. But as you well know, that piano was that. Not so much as a pair of underwear otherwise. And out of respect for her, or maybe just to keep the peace, he finally relented. I'll guarantee you one thing—he never said a word about it to me or anybody else. I've always respected him for that. It was your mama that told me all this. She said she didn't even want him buying y'all groceries."

This was true. Taftly and his mother had gone for years on little more than macaroni-and-cheese, fried pork chops, rice with tomato gravy, apple sauce, and chicken pot pies, the last far and away the sentimental favorite. They were two pudgy people in a tiny World War II house with Glenn Miller albums, library books and chicken pot pies. One of the things Taftly had liked best about visiting his granddaddy was the chance to actually consume a steak and french fries.

"I remember every bit of it because my marriage was coming undone about that time."

Taftly knew the story well. Jim Bates had left the practice of law to go to seminary. He believed he'd been called by God to do so but forgot to check with his wife first, who assumed she and God were co-captains running her husband's life. When he started work at First Baptist as assistant pastor, with an assistant pastor's salary, constantly carting seniors and kiddies to church functions, having to smile a lot, she left him. "Just pretend I've been ruptured," she said. "Raptured," Pastor Bates corrected, though she paid him no mind.

Her departure had been public and angry, leaving the new

assistant pastor to wander the streets of town like some lost circus bear.

"I'm sorry about that," Taftly said.

Pastor Bates shrugged him off. "One I mainly felt sorry for was your granddaddy. Your grandmama had died a few years before you were born and he was counting on your daddy sticking around. Not that he tried to make him. But the curious thing about your daddy was that he genuinely liked it just fine in Copiah Springs. He was small-town through and through. Hated cities. Loved the idea of picking up in the same place as *his* daddy and granddaddy and carrying right on. All he wanted was a year or two abroad. Then he wanted right back here. Its funny how things turn out."

Taftly's eyes were softer, attentive. Pastor Bates went on: "I believe your granddaddy got pretty lonesome. Those years were hard on him. I don't like to think about it to tell the truth."

They thought of it. Then Pastor Bates fixed Taftly with a firm stare. Taftly realized he was doing the best he could and would continue to whether Taftly thought so or not. It humbled Taftly.

"Life is long," Pastor Bates said softly.

Taftly was going to add something to this, maybe put in a word about suffering, the length and breadth of it and the great endurance that was required to make it safely to the grave, but Pastor Bates continued talking.

"Few weeks ago, we had us a revival. A good one. 'Bout the

middle of the week, these two girls came down the aisle, wanting to give their hearts to Jesus. Man, they were crying up a storm, really boo-hooing. Make-up running everywhere. It was a sight. Said they'd done something that couldn't be forgiven. You'd of thought their lives were over and they weren't any older than you, can you imagine that?"

Taftly leaned forward as if his head were too heavy for him, his lips parted hotly from dread and panic.

"I never got the bottom line on it. People say stuff like that all the time. There's two kinds of people that's lost—those who think they can't be forgiven and those who think they don't need to be forgiven. The latter kind are idiots, but the others I worry about. Anyhow, I finally convinced those girls God could forgive them for whatever they'd done and they prayed the sinner's prayer. Great big girls. Not real easy to look at. And mean as hell I bet. But God forgave 'em just the same."

Taftly was standing. The heat in the room had become unbearable, and he was standing to get clear of it. "Do you know where my father is?"

"I'm not for sure. Last I heard from him he said he was going to get in touch with you. It's why I wanted to have this talk. You haven't heard from him?"

"Nope."

"That's strange."

"Not to me."

Pastor Bates walked around the desk. The pits of his shirt were marked with a heavy sweat, but all Taftly noticed were his large hands. They should have been the hands of a father. Taftly's heart caught thinking of how it wasn't so when they reached out to take him in.

XIV

DENNIS CONSIDERED THE COPIAH HARPER College library to be insufficient for his researches, not to mention his talents, but it was the only library available to him. Earlier that year he'd been permanently booted from the town library for having made himself the plague of the periodical section. Once a week he'd been in the habit of arriving sharply at eight in the morning to greet the town librarian, occasionally scolding her for running late. By noon he would still be there, with magazines and newspapers piled around him. Hunger pains usually took hold at that point, causing Dennis to grow quarrelsome and to take issue with everything he read, frequently aloud, until one day a group of angry mothers insisted he be removed for good.

Which was fine with Dennis. In his opinion, it was a small library for small minds. He'd already defeated every book there anyway. "Not a book here I ain't got the better of," he'd remarked on his way out the door.

One thing the college library had going for it was college girls. If Dennis hadn't been engaged in such a serious enterprise, he could have done something about them. As it was, he had work to do. He'd already tried out the internet, but a search on Taftly Harper hadn't produced for him. There was plenty about Copiah Harper College and he'd even found an article written by Taftly's granddaddy for a hunting magazine, but Taftly himself scored a zero. "Not for long," Dennis promised as he exited the information superhighway.

A bewildered foreign student had helped Dennis figure out the computer, but as her English was iffy, Dennis had no choice but to confront the head librarian directly in order to continue. He took a moment to study the woman before making his approach. She seemed a little too satisfied with herself, he decided, something that would change when she realized he was in the process of making literary history.

"May I help you?"

Dennis pitched her a smile straightaway, a little something on the house is how he thought of it. He read her name tag. He liked name tags and wished he had one. "I'd be pleased if you would, Mrs. Woodley," he told her.

"What can I do?"

Dennis decided he liked Mrs. Woodley after all. She had a warm warbling voice, not unlike the stooped woman who had the cooking show on television. From this alone he could tell she was top-shelf, a good quality for someone who had to manage tall stacks of books. *Top shelf!* Dennis, Dennis said to himself, you're good, a regular wordsworth, or was that smith?

"Is there a certain book you're looking for?"

"No, no. But I'm dealing with something highly sensitive right now. Do you have a sound-proof conference room where we could discuss it mano-a-womano?"

It was then that Mrs. Woodley realized she'd actually heard of Dennis before. In fact, she'd been warned about him, though she had to admit he exceeded his reputation. "No, I'm afraid we don't," she said.

"Well, I don't want this to get out to the general public. People can get very excited when you start waving red meat in front a their faces."

"Oh, I imagine so."

Dennis frowned but believed he could trust Mrs. Woodley. She had Dennis's favorite kind of eyes, blue. They were closely set, like a bird's, which Dennis believed denoted both shrewdness and song. And she wore a blue dress to match them. She wasn't too big or too small and she wasn't too old or too young. Thinking this reminded Dennis of something, but he couldn't figure what.

"Anyway, we just don't have a conference room. But I promise to keep our discussion under wraps," Mrs. Woodley assured Dennis.

"Well, all right. See, the thing is, I'm combining a very potent combination of brain powers. Never been done before. You've heard of yer geniuses. And you've heard of yer biographers. And the one mixes with the other, right?"

Mrs. Woodley pushed her chair back from the desk and crossed her arms.

"But what ya ain't heard of is a genius biographer writing about a genius. Which if ya do the math is as simple as one plus one. Ya get a third genius, being the work in progress, right?"

"I suppose that would be correct."

"So that's my particular cross to bear. I've got two geniuses and am fixin to make a third. Now the first, let's call him genius number one, he ain't on the internet. There's no information about him at all. See that's where I'm breaking new ground. It ain't easy, and I need all the information I can get."

"I see."

"And remember this. It ain't a typical biography. And not just because of the combination of geniuses. It's going to be multi-media oriented. There's the part I write, then the audio, which I already got plenty a that, don't you worry. So first I market them two and with the proceeds maybe add video. That makes three again." Dennis held up two fingers and a thumb to be certain Mrs. Woodley made the connection. "I need more information is the bottom line."

Mrs. Woodley believed her best bet was to simply help Dennis and then send him on his way. "It seems to me," she began. She put her pencil to her lip and thought. "Yes, seems to me as if you are to be someone's Boswell."

Dennis nodded expertly. He wondered what a Boswell was. It sounded like a computer.

"James Boswell wrote perhaps the greatest biography of all time, you see. It was about the life of Samuel Johnson. And like you, he had to start from scratch. So forget about libraries. Libraries just won't do."

"Naw, I guess they won't." Dennis rubbed his chin thoughtfully. "How did old Boswell do it?"

"He recorded everything Johnson said."

"Good god! Everything?"

"Well, he recorded quite a lot. You have to remember, Johnson was perhaps the greatest genius of all time."

"Yeah. Johnson. I bet they thought they had them quite a combination going, them two. But think on one little detail, my dear Mrs. Woodley—some of us alive ain't dead yet. Ain't over till its over."

"You have a point there."

"Sharp one, too." Dennis flexed his biceps. He disguised this with a yawn but was sure Mrs. Woodley got the message. When he finished, he placed his hands on the desk and leaned forward. "But see, my problem is, I can't follow genius number one around with my recorder," he whispered. "He might not like it. Matter a fact, I know he wouldn't."

"Boswell didn't use a recorder. He wrote down what Johnson said by hand."

"Wrote it down by hand, eh? Old school. Just followed Johnson around and wrote down what he said."

"That's right."

"It's a wonder Johnson never got tired of him." Dennis considered this. "Everything he said, huh?"

"Well, he wrote about his life and times, his impressions of Johnson. He definitely inserted himself into the process. It was Boswell's Johnson, after all. "

"I'm inserting myself, too. Count on that."

"Sounds promising."

"Now let me ask you this. Did some of Boswell's Johnson come from his following Johnson around in secret?"

"Oh, my! I'm not sure about that!" Mrs. Woodley began to giggle. "Grubbing about Grub Street. Worming his way into Johnson's vast interior. Like a mole." Then she stopped giggling. "Now wait a minute. That was early Johnson, not late. I don't think he was much around Grub Street in his later years. Hm."

At last Dennis had identified Mrs. Woodley's flaw. She was dotty. You could sign that right on the dotted line. Dennis had to chuckle because he'd done it again, been clever. How hard it was going to be for him to wait for the world to learn of his wit and wisdom.

"But think on this, Mrs. Woodley. If somebody had been following Johnson around in secret, think how much better it would have been. That would have been the untold story. Think if someone could tell an untold story. Now that would be something."

Mrs. Woodley had to agree. "I agree," she said. "That would indeed be something." If Mrs. Woodley had had another life to live, she might have consented to spend another few minutes with Dennis, but as she possessed only the one life, she needed to hurry him along. She stood and hoped the phone would ring.

"Well, Ma'am. That's what I'm all about. Telling the untold story. In secret. It's where Boswell missed the boat, right where I'm dropping anchor. Uncharted territory an' what not. 'Cause if genius number two not only records genius number one, but furthermore begins to follow him around in secret an to jot down impressions, then what ya got is a real improvement over things."

"You might be right," Mrs. Woodley said. She patted the desk top. "Good luck to you." And be on your way.

"What ya got is something getting close to a *totality*." What a word, Dennis thought. Why not say it again? "Yep. A toe-tality."

"Mm."

"From all angles and in between. if you follow."

"Yes. I believe I do."

"I know you do." Dennis gave Mrs. Woodley a second gratis smile. He tried to tip his hat but it was stuck, so he saluted. "You might even get you a mention, young lady."

Mrs. Woodley touched her throat. "Oh dear. Well, good luck again."

As Dennis walked away, Mrs. Woodley removed her hand from her throat, though she now felt a slight lump in it. Dennis Jolly struck her as a man who had something to offer the world if only someone in the world had the patience to endure him. But where in the world did such a person exist?

Of course, she reflected, she was prone toward sentimentality, and the cold truth of the matter may have been that Dennis was simply to be avoided at all costs. She sighed. One thing was for sure, she felt very sorry for Dennis Jolly's Johnson.

XV

THE WEEK BEFORE THANKSGIVING Taftly walked out by the pond to find Dennis digging a pit on the far side. The shoveling was furious, perhaps even criminal in its intensity. *Dear God, he's killed somebody*, Taftly thought.

Dennis worked steadily, jawing a tremendous chaw while tossing impressive amounts of dirt over his shoulder, his countenance bright and able. Taftly watched closely and feared the hole might be intended for three or four people. A regrettable humming arose from the pit as well, bringing to mind a cringing hostage playing kazoo at gun point. When Dennis began changing octaves abruptly, the sudden ranges so offended Taftly that he stepped forward to stop the terrible noise.

"You digging a hole to China?"

Dennis abated with a cloying wail of agony. "Sure feels like it." He began slinging great drams of sweat in all directions, after which he threw the shovel to the ground and proceeded to stretch his hamstrings.

Taftly had seen this before and deplored it. Dennis, to be certain onlookers were cognizant of his flexibility, would cock his heel nearly to his ear with a look of vengeance. So positioned, he'd press the more until tearful, grunting barbarically, as if he were presently to savage a village. "Wouldn't want to pull a hammy," he'd explain when capable.

Taftly was going to ask about the hole again when Dennis disappeared into it. "Look out," he warned from below. His intention was to spring from it in a single bound, cat-like, but instead he gained the lip only to discover his reserve of inertia had been exhausted. A sheer panic settled over his face before he toppled backward. Wretched groans followed. Taftly covered his mouth to keep from laughing.

"I landed on the fanny pack," Dennis cried.

"Oh, dear. You all right?"

"'Spect so. Ain't nothing's killed me yet."

"No. I expect not." Taftly leaned down and offered Dennis a hand. "So what are you doing, anyhow?"

"Work fer one thang. Seems like I'm the onliest one to get a damned thang done round here. Be glad this hole ain't waiting on Clem is all I got to say."

Though Dennis claimed for himself the title of groundskeeper, the grounds were in fact kept by a stout man named Clementine Jeffries. Dennis did not like Clementine because of this and Clementine, for his part, disapproved of Dennis in the extreme. He found him shiftless, the walking breathing image of how his own equally shiftless sons thought of white people. Dennis was the punk of a white man they had in mind when they penned their verboten rap lyrics of no quality whatsoever. Of course, Clementine reflected, had Dennis showed up at the house one afternoon his sons would have run for their lives. This made him giggle, but not enough to give a shit for Dennis, who would watch him work the yard over each Saturday with a critical eye as if he were an overseer.

Clementine liked Taftly, however. When Taftly had quit his job at Copiah Springs Water, he'd taken to playing the market with some of his inheritance. Clementine asked about this one day and Taftly said he'd play some for him. He did, successfully. Soon Clementine was bringing actual money of his own for Taftly to invest and then he brought a friend of his who said he was a bluesman and had killed some honkeys with a butcher knife who deserved it. Taftly thought maybe the bluesman needed to be decapitated where he stood. "What's that supposed to mean?" he asked.

"Don't lose my money, motherfucker," the man growled.

He called himself Big House Bradley, though he weighed perhaps a hundred pounds. He resembled nothing so much as a dog turd with a hat. His ears were bunched yet razorous, like an elfs. Clementine was ashamed for having brought the sorry son-of-a-bitch over, bluesman or not.

"Don't lose your money? You gave me a check for ten dollars," Taftly cried. "Probably a bad one."

"You calling me out?" Big House wanted to know.

"I'll fucking lay yo ass out right here if you don't shut the fuck up right now this fucking instant," Clementine was explaining. He had a sickle in his hand and meant it. Though in his sixties, Clementine had the build of a much younger man. His sclerotic eyes bulged and his skin seemed stretched back. In fact, his face appeared as if it were testing some speed limit and barely holding. Even his hair receded in haste.

He brought the sickle up for Big House to see. It looked almost miniature in Clementine's enormous hands. Whenever Clementine pointed or gestured, Taftly's eyes were swept hard in whatever direction his fingers indicated, following far along the intended path.

"Come over to Tafly house and ack like a goddamned yard ape," Clementine grumbled.

"That's racist, motherfucker. If we was in Chicago—"

"Motherfucker, we ain't in Chicago. We in Tafly's yard and I want you to apologize right this fucking minute fo I whack yo goddamned head off. Den we see what kinda blues you sing."

"I ain't sorry," Big House whispered. "What you lookin at?" he asked Taftly. Big House was hunched now, almost disappearing in his shirt.

Taftly felt queasy but angry. He'd be damned if he'd make Big House any money. His granddaddy, God bless his soul, would have forbidden it. "You've mistaken me for someone who gives a shit about my life," Taftly announced. He said it suddenly and with force. It shocked the three of them and no one doubted it.

"Well, shit," Big House said.

When Taftly tore the check up, Clementine slapped Big House across the back of the head. "See what you done, nigger. Made Tafly sorry to be alive."

As soon as Clementine and Big House were gone, Dennis arrived with grave importance, hardly clothed and scabrous. "They give ya any trouble?" he asked. "Just let me know, partner." Dennis chopped the air in front of Taftly's face, just missing his nose.

"I need to be alone," Taftly told him.

"No problemo," Dennis scooted a few feet away and continued the karate. "I'm not sure 'bout ol' Clem though. Noticed him slackin a bit. He don't seem to want to work. I'd keep an eye on him."

"That's what he says about you," Taftly snapped.

"Says what?"

"That I ought to keep an eye on you."

Taftly kept an eye on the piles of fresh dirt, thinking of Clementine. He smiled. A few risky trades had just paid big and Clementine was in for some good news for Thanksgiving.

"Makin' us a barbecue pit is what I'm doing," Dennis shouted. "*Hey, makin' us a barbecue pit!*" He snapped his fingers to get Taftly's attention. "I *said* I'm slaving over a barbecue pit if anybody cares."

"A what?"

"Done bought us a pig and everthang. Ain't got plans for Thanksgiving have ya?"

Taftly squinted. "No," he said. He took a step back, dazed. "No I guess not."

"Well, you do now."

XVI

TAFTLY WAS DEEP INTO HIS CUPS before he could fully credit what was occurring, that he and Dennis were barbecuing a pig for Thanksgiving dinner and that for some deeply perplexing reason his heart had actually quickened with gratitude when Dennis told him of the plans. How strangely appropriate the night seemed, invincible in its simplicity and unexpectedness. As warm grumbles of bourbon filled his stomach, Taftly took curious pleasure from the fact that he could be content with someone like Dennis Jolly on a holiday.

Dennis had purchased a set of chaise lounge chairs for the event. He believed this remarked an extravagance suitable for a man of his distinction. Regular folding chairs were not sufficient in his opinion and he was determined that he and Taftly would recline beside the large pit in wicker splendor like two bumpkin pharaohs. And there they sat, tending the fire and drinking whisky. After the bottle had made several rounds, Taftly found that Dennis was beginning to look almost human in the firelight.

"This here's something my old daddy never would've done, I'll guarantee that," Dennis stated, feeling Taftly's gaze.

A log popped as Dennis absently churned the crackling embers with a broom handle he'd brought with him. Taftly watched quietly.

"No sir," Dennis continued, shaking his head. "I don't reckon this was his cup of coffee."

"He didn't like to barbecue?" Taftly asked.

"I'm sure he liked it just fine," Dennis said, chuckling. "What he didn't like all that much was me."

"You?"

"Which I can understand. Don't get me wrong. I annoy hell outta people sometimes." Dennis cogitated on this. "And sometimes I annoy people all the time," he added.

"No you . . ." Taftly quit his lie. He felt the generous fib would only wound Dennis further. "Well, shit, Dennis," he whispered finally.

"You hit the nail on the tail there, partner." Dennis stuck his lips out, harassing the embers with renewed vigor. "But it's because I'm alone all the time. And when I do get to talk to people, they mostly ignore me. Burns me up and makes me talk more. You don't talk back to me and you better believe I'm gonna talk back to you."

Dennis removed his cap and eased his fingers through his stringy hair. It was to be a significantly weary motion, but he'd become so excited he raked his scalp as if to tear it loose from his skull. "Talk, talk, talk," he continued. "I bore my own self. I hear myself talking and sometimes I can't hardly stand it. I *need*, I say I *need*, me a button to push that'd blow my head off. That'd show me."

Taftly had never heard Dennis speak as sensibly. He sounded quite normal, his voice sure and resolved.

"What do you mean your father never liked you," Taftly ventured, knowing to his bones exactly what Dennis meant.

"Just what I said. He was ashamed of me. Him and my mama both run off on me. 'Cept that wadn't even my real mama. My real mama's still up in Memphis. Smoking. 'What ya doing, Mama?' Smoking. Shit. Her idea of a Thanksgiving is a merry chase on the highball train with a caboose full a Marlboro Reds. Heaven would be God giving her an extra mouth or two so she could really get busy with them Reds, set some kind of record." Dennis lit the cigarette he'd been rolling. "She run off on my daddy when I was little so I don't know her all that well other than the cigarette part."

"You ever visit?"

"Yeah. And give her cigarettes. I put one a them exploding fire crackers in one a her Reds one time and the damn thing nearly blew her lips off. Know what she said? Nothing. Just relit the damn thing and kept on smoking. I'd bet my bottom dollar she'll live to be a hunnerd and collect on my will and smoke that up." Dennis shook his head. "But anyhow, after she run off, my daddy found him another little ole gal and they fled me long 'bout the sixth grade. Left me to my aunt. She wadn't all that crazy about me neither. Course she was uglier than hell."

Taftly stepped over to hand Dennis the bottle, then settled again watching the fire. Its low flames warmed something deep inside him, drawing him out and making him friendly. He recalled hunting trips with his granddaddy and roaring talk by the campfire late into the night. Whisky and a good fire could open a man up, even a hard man, and Taftly knew that it had always been so. *Maybe I should give Dennis my old car,* he mused.

"But I had me one good year," Dennis announced.

"During childhood?"

"No, during my whole life. And that one didn't last but a few weeks."

"Your one good year?"

"Yeah. Wanna hear about it?"

"Sure."

"Well, 'bout the end of high school, I'd done saved up some money. I'd worked two jobs since junior high and had me a nice little savings. One day I was walking past the used car lot and saw this M.G. Turned out I had enough money so I bought it. After that, when I wadn't working, I was driving. This was before all the cares of life had spoiled my looks. I might even could've given you a good run for the money in them days. I used to drive women plumb crazy, I mean flat out *torment* 'em."

Taftly ignored this comment. "Was this in Memphis?" he asked.

"Just the other side of the Mississippi line. Yep. Here partner."

When Dennis leaned to hand Taftly the bottle he realized that his arm wasn't long enough. Since he was already bent over, he began to crawl, approaching Taftly like some piteous being stricken by the gods in a Greek tragedy, head agog, moving forward in embarrassed increments, earthbound. Neither Dennis nor Taftly knew why Dennis had decided to crawl like this but both were deeply ashamed of it. Such hideousness threatened to break the spell of the hearth Taftly had been savoring, and he swigged hard to regain it while Dennis scuttled back to his spot in turmoil.

Having demeaned himself, Dennis craved a terrific lie. He was on the verge of saying something about how he'd taught Elvis to ride bare-back like an indian when it occurred to him that he may as well see about the pig. "Saw Elvis a few times," he mumbled. "That was back when he was in his prime."

"When I was little, I always wanted to be Elvis. I used to sing along to my mother's old forty-fives," Taftly said, trying to be helpful.

Dennis turned the pig once around, grinning. He'd seen Taftly gamboling about the cabin in his mother's night gown and was glad to learn that Taftly wasn't as bent as he'd first suspected. As soon as he had the chance, he would have to correct his notes on this point. Maybe Taftly was imitating Elvis, something Dennis could understand.

"That so. Hey, by-the-by, I had me a chance to join the

Memphis Mafia." Dennis winced but his need was overpowering. "Yeah. They made you go through a karate test and I laid that Italian-looking sombitch low. Pissed him off. Voted me out after that. But ol' Elvis coulda used me. Boy they goofed that one up."

Taftly looked away without comment. He knew Dennis had berthed a whopper and felt badly for him.

Dennis felt badly for Dennis, too, but as Taftly had looked away, he had been handed an opportunity he could not refuse. He discretely removed his note pad from his shirt pocket and readied his ball-point pen. "So what about yer formative years there, Taftster?"

"My *what?*"

"You know, formative years."

"What do you mean? And what are you doing with that note pad?"

"Sketches. I like to sketch nature."

"At night?"

"What's wrong with the night?"

It was a beautiful night, as a matter of fact. Every few minutes a cool wind swept the pond, fluttering bay, oak, and pecan leaves, twirling the loosest ones down as if to garnish this rare communion. The stars were far but clear, rotating in their vast blue fold like spun spurs. Taftly could almost hear them clicking. He decided to concentrate on them and not to think about Dennis wondering about his formative years. "That pig's starting to smell good," Taftly said.

"It'll eat I bet." Dennis placed the pen and paper on the ground and took out his knife. He searched for a place to carve. "He's a smug one. See that expression?"

"Wouldn't mess with him yet. He's not cooked and he's too hot."

"Hell, a little piece won't do much damage. I got a stomach strong as an iron tea cup." Dennis plopped a shred of pork in his mouth and shrieked girlishly, spitting the sizzling meat to the ground. "Shit amighty that's hot!"

"Told you." Taftly lay back listening to the leaves, thinking what he could make of them. They rattled up from the ground in building cadences, arriving at crescendos that made him think of giddy young primas rushing onto the stage before their cues. "That pig's got a ways to go," Taftly reminded.

"Sure is smug for the shape he's in." Dennis didn't know if he liked the pig anymore. Its gruesomely sealed lips had charred into a smile. He wanted to whack it a few good times over the head with the broomstick but thought this would give him away as a lunatic. "Anyhow, about that one good year."

"Yeah. What happened?"

"Got me a girl's what happened, buddy boy. A good one, too. Carted her around all that summer. She was something. Then she split on me. Know why?"

"Why?"

"Somebody told on me."

"Told on you?"

"Yeah."

Taftly waited for Dennis to continue, but he did not. Instead, he began to roll another cigarette with forlorn care, as if the act were merely a lifeless discipline, all that was left for him, a mortally wounded soldier marching forward toward no destination whatsoever and besides that alone.

"Told on you how?" Taftly asked.

"Some boys went over there and told on me. *Told on me*," Dennis repeated impatiently.

"And it got you in trouble?"

"Well of course. That was the end of it pure and simple. Did me in. And I loved that girl. She was the only true love of my life, matter of fact. I think sometimes we might could've amounted to something together. Anyhow, that was how the good year ended."

The story touched Taftly, but he could not allow the mystery of it to prosper for another moment. What exactly had the boys told on Dennis? He was going to ask about this directly when for some reason it occurred to him that he'd been drinking after Dennis the night long—Dennis, who although apparently human, was still Dennis. He remembered there were two tin coffee cups in the leather satchel he'd brought with him and retrieved them and tossed one Dennis's way. "Forgot I brought these," he said.

"Getting fancy now."

"May as well pull out all the stops."

"Yank up the starts, too!" Dennis barely got this out before being whiplashed by his own laughter.

Taftly shook his head. Dennis was beginning to remind him of Dennis again. In doing so, he was beginning to remind Taftly of Taftly in an unwanted way. He thought a cigarette might staunch this unseemly progression and sparked a clove. He slackened his wrist dramatically and drew from it with his palm pressed to his cheek. He wasn't sure why but it pleased him.

When Dennis emerged from his convulsions to study this affected bit of silliness, he could not resist trying the procedure out himself. As soon as Taftly caught him at this, he struck home.

"What do you mean *told on you?*" Taftly demanded. "Told *what* on you?"

"Told her who I was, what ya think? Told her the whole Dennis Jolly story, epic and all. Course, I guess it *was me.* There wadn't no getting around *that.* They told on me but I reckon they was just telling the truth."

"Well," Taftly said.

"Yeah. Well. What else can ya say? Truth's the truth. Boy she was a sexy lil ole thang, though. Legs for days. Hell, for weeks. What about you?"

"Me what?"

Dennis believed it would help him best Boswell if he could get news of Taftly's sexual history. He probably wouldn't use it *per se*, but it would assist him in constructing a more plausible psychological profile. So far, his Boswelling had been burdensome, mainly because he didn't have a car. When Taftly went into town he had to thumb a ride or walk in order to spy out impressions of Taftly's life and times. It wasn't any easier when Taftly stayed home, either, since Taftly often kept his curtains drawn. Drunken Taftly could sometimes be cooperative, especially at night, but as he'd sadly noted earlier, even drunk Taftly had become quiet and shifty. As Dennis already had several hours of quality audio, he didn't think that was much of a problem. What he needed now was more information for his written commentary. That meant more surveillance of sober Taftly in order to produce a true totality.

But Dennis's Johnson was tricky. To Dennis's mind, Taftly was obsessed with privacy, which made beating Boswell that much harder. From the way Mrs. Woodley described things, Boswell's Johnson was a real talker. To be quite honest, Dennis sometimes wished he'd never heard of Boswell and Johnson. They were getting in his way, almost provoking him. It would have been good if both of them had been flattened by a truck while they were running their big fat mouths. If Dennis had known about their project in time, he might could have arranged that. Still, Dennis wouldn't give up just because there was unfair competition. He would have to work harder, that was all. For now, he would have to ply Taftly with generous conversation in order to lure him into revealing himself.

"Me what, Dennis?"

Dennis had it. He wouldn't use the word sex and thus his intentions would remain covert. And instead of asking about Taftly's first sexual experience, he'd skip to the second causing Taftly to doubt there was any rhyme or reason to his queries.

"Romance is what, old boy."

"Oh. Romance. Not much to tell."

"What about your second romantic involvement?"

"My second what?"

"Your second. Second time you...had romance."

Taftly looked over angrily. Dennis tried to hide the note pad and succeeded in looking like a person trying to hide a note pad. "I really don't want to talk about *romance*," Taftly said. He was now thoroughly agitated. What if Dennis knew about the Clydesdales? Why had he specifically asked about his *second* romance? Surely the Clydesdales hadn't told anyone what had happened. Or had they? Or was Dennis simply being Dennis? Taftly sat up straight and finished his drink. Next thing, he'll ask about my *third* romance.

"My third was my best," Dennis managed weakly.

"That's it. What do you mean? What do you mean third?" Taftly was standing.

"No, no, no. I didn't mean anything. I just don't get much opportunity to talk. It's like I told ya. I didn't mean nothing."

Dennis hoped Taftly wouldn't leave. He wanted to throw his note pad in the fire and then maybe himself. He deserved it. Taftly had been so decent to him, and he hated to think he might scare him off like he did every one else. He'd worked so hard to have a proper Thanksgiving and now he was on the verge of ruining it. "Please just ignore me," he said.

Taftly felt he had over-reacted. He'd been rude. Dennis was only trying to have a conversation. "I'm sorry," he said.

"I'm the one that's sorry."

Taftly sat down again. "No, I was rude."

"Believe me, I'm the one that's sorry."

"Sometime you should just ignore *me*," Taftly said.

Dennis dragged his chaise lounge chair closer to Taftly. He unscrewed the bottle cap ceremoniously and poured them full cups. "To my one good year," he said.

"To better years," Taftly said.

Dennis leaned back. He wondered if this would be a good time to teach Taftly something, perhaps a little primer on the nearness of God. It was good being Taftly's pal. It was good to have a pal period, but Taftly made him proud.

"About my romances. I haven't had much of a love life, so I'm a bit touchy. Don't take it personally. You can ask me things, I'm just not promising I'll answer."

"I understand. I shouldn't have asked, period. Hey, you ever been married?"

Taftly smiled. Dennis was impossible. "No. Never been married."

"But you been close."

"Not really. You?"

"'Fraid I have."

Taftly jerked his head over, astonished. He'd asked the question simply to be polite and could hardly credit the answer he'd been given. "You were *married*. Married, married," he went on.

"Preacher did it to me," Dennis said. "It didn't turn out so good, neither. We didn't really love each other for one thing. I didn't like the way she looked, and she didn't like the way I looked for another. That's to say nothing of how we felt about each other's personalities. But we were working together washing dishes in this restaurant down on the coast. I don't know. We just did it. Bunny was her name. She didn't act like no bunny, by god."

"What happened?"

"Some business man found her and took her off of me. I found out later why. He had him some perversions, and she did 'em to him. Like I said, she wadn't no looker, but she could do all the perversions."

"Perversions?"

"Oh, yeah. Plural. She wrote me about the whole thing from Phoenix, Arizona. That's where he carried her off to. It was something about salt water taffy and duck feathers. Damnation, it was sick. And what else was sick was that she told all of this on a post card, and at the end of it said not to tell nobody else about it. On a post card. Bunny wadn't too bright."

"Why did she tell you all that?"

"So as not to hurt my feelings. She figured a story like that'd make me get over her pretty quick."

"Did it?"

"I reckon I didn't have no choice. But I sure had got used to having somebody to come home to at night. Bunny. Ought to have named her Hyena. We never even got divorced. Didn't have no money. I reckon it don't really matter one way or the other with people like me and Bunny. But hell, sometimes I almost miss her."

Taftly watched Dennis stir the ashes. His cap was crooked, though his T-shirt had been ironed and starched. One of the temples to his glasses had come off. It was hard to envision a woman putting her arms around Dennis, much less kissing him. "I'm sorry," Taftly said softly.

"Aw, it's all right." Dennis dropped the stick. "Hey, I almost forgot!"

He jumped up and ran into his shack cackling. Taftly watched him return with a bucket from which he began scattering handfuls of corn. He walked all around the pond doing this. He pitched some toward Taftly, who ducked under his quilt.

"What are you doing?"

"May as well be Thanksgiving for everbody," Dennis explained. "I was thinking it'd be something if there was a whole bunch of birds around here in the morning while we get things ready. Just aflying everywheres. Like confetti."

The sun had just cleared the horizon when Dennis shook Taftly awake. Before his eyes could focus he heard the riotous clamor of several hundred birds fighting over the corn. A coon examined the crazed scene indignantly from the tree line and turned back into the woods. The wind had grown stronger and colder and birds swooped recklessly through hectic upheavals of leaves as the pig surrendered a succulent aroma. *A regular Thanksgiving melee*, Taftly conceded.

Before noon the eastern sky had darkened and columns of rain were advancing. Taftly and Dennis carried the pig to the porch, spreading it over newspapers. Dennis had filled four serving plates with meat when his arm gave out. "Oh, god amighty! My arm's done give out!" he hollered, not two feet away from Taftly.

They were in the chaise lounge chairs giving thanks by early afternoon. Taftly had prepared a potato salad with red onions and dill. He'd cooked some collards and made his mother's sausage stuffing along with some rolls. He and Dennis had nothing more to say after a while and drank and ate contentedly, growing blissfully tired, Dennis rousing himself every so often to spread more corn. At some point, Dennis sawed the pig's head off and staked it atop his old television antennae, which he drove into the ground on the near side of the pond. Taftly was too exhausted to ask why and believed it didn't matter one way or the other anyway.

By the time the first drops of rain splattered the tin roof, they were thick into dreams. Dennis's snoozing visage looked something like a benign scarecrow's head made by a preening diligent girl scout with repressed wants of love. Taftly's mouth had connected with the floor of the porch by way of a strand of drool. They snored.

The storm clouds eventually pushed west and the fading sun rimmed even the darkest of them with a marvelous amber sheen as the rinsed air lent the sky the aspect of primal twilight. A few remaining birds quietly picked over the yard for stray kernels. The pig's head shook in the wind, snubbing everything. Classified ads and front pages traversed the ground as if teased up by puppet strings. An empty whisky bottle lay on the porch steps. The coon returned and rushed the trimmings, tipping the potato salad over, though not before making off with the tray of rolls. The scene was calamitous, the wrecked litter of a sacked village, but there on the porch sat Taftly Harper and Dennis Jolly, arms folded neatly, like two children spared from the plunder by the unfathomable mercy of God.

XVII

DECEMBER BROUGHT MORE RAIN AND COLD weather.
The sky brooded daily, punishing everything beneath her
bruised expanse with grim colors. The change hit Taftly
squarely and put him down. All possible consolations shim-
mered just beyond his grasp, which somehow reminded him
of the Christmas ornaments he vowed not to put up or even
acknowledge.

Not Dennis. His roof had become a clotted mass of twinkling lights of every conceivable shade. He'd covered his windows with faux snow and could no longer see out them. Tinsel
lay about his porch in messy piles like the random leavings of
a metallic dog bearing up under a severe case of dysentery.

What was more, Dennis had begun to traffic in a hurried
euphoria. It started the day the postman delivered an enormous brown box which Dennis signed for and then carried
into the shack by way of an uncertain hunching gait. It looked
as if Dennis were attempting to hump the thing and the

beastly coitus-travel made Taftly wonder if there were a mail-order bride inside.

Dennis would not reveal the contents, and for the first time Taftly noticed he began to lock his door. Formerly everywhere and unwanted, Dennis now remained in his shack for hours. In weaker moments, Taftly fancied he missed Dennis. Eventually Taftly came to believe Dennis was actually neglecting him. He envied Dennis's industry and purpose, whatever it was he was doing, unless, of course, what he was doing was laboring atop a thirteen-year-old Filipino.

After a few days like this, Taftly became ravenous for company. He wanted to see Fay arrive in a box, by god, naked save for a flimsy trailer-trash tank-top which he would dispose of with a growl. Though he'd sworn off trips to her house—a sort of Christmas present for everyone involved—he soon realized his resolution wouldn't last. The breaking point came when he received a package from the state penitentiary.

Taftly found the padded envelope in his mailbox late one evening. He strolled to his porch, figuring some convict had gotten a bad address. Taftly absently tore the package open. He found a note, then he heard something fall to the floor. It was a mood ring. The stone was black as Train's heart.

Dear Motherfucker, esq. (Don't try and act like I'm not educated you piece of shit, I know to use esquire.)

Please put the ring on to tell your fortune. If its black, your dead. If its green, your dead. If its brown, your dead. If its kind

of blue and green, your still dead. Any other color and I'll rip
you're head off and shit down you're neck.

You'rs Very Truly,

R. Train.

Taftly ripped the note apart and rushed to Dennis's shack. He
knocked and then knocked harder. Nothing. He tried to open
the door but it was locked. "Open up, damnit!" he cried.
"Open up! Its an emergency!"

Taftly heard a prolific and tortured commotion, ample
grunting and scuttling about.

"What the hell?" Dennis said, cracking the door.

"I got to ask you a question."

"I'm busy."

Taftly's eyes swelled with indignation. "*You're* busy! *You!*
You're telling me *you're* busy!"

"In English. What language you want?"

Taftly took a step forward but Dennis blocked him. "I want
to come in."

"Cain't right now. Got a project going."

They stared at one another, both quite shocked at their
respective positions.

"May I speak with you out here for a moment then?" Taftly
asked.

Dennis rubbed his chin, wallowing in this rare superiority.
"Well, for a *moment*," he allowed.

"Fine. I have a question. About the training, the fighting,

I'm coming along right?"

"Sure fire."

"I mean I've improved."

"Oh, yeah. You've got the makings of a champion I'd say. And I ought to know."

"But you think I'm ready to take somebody."

Dennis giggled. "Whoo! Sure!"

"All right. That's all I wanted to know."

Taftly began walking back to the house when Dennis called after him. "Just one bit of advice," he said. "I wouldn't pick on nobody my own size."

Taftly phoned the sheriff to be certain that Train had not escaped. As far as Sheriff Williams knew, Train remained in the pokey. Taftly still believed he should go and tell Fay about receiving the package, however, or at least have a look around the neighborhood to be sure she was safe.

"Dennis! Open up!"

"What now?"

"Call the state penitentiary and ask if a man named Rodney Train is still there."

"Are you serious?"

"Yes I'm serious. Do it!"

"All right. But it's gonna be long distance."

"I'll pay you back. Just do it. I've got to go."

It was just shy of midnight when Taftly parked on Fay's street. He rolled down the window, feeling the cold with his hand. Fay would not likely venture out on such a night. Taftly hoped not anyway, else she and the chap might catch cold. He chewed his lip for awhile, flexing his muscles and wondering what Train's first move would be if he were to escape.

Presently he was deep into his imagination, in a front yard much like Fay's, though this front yard was skillfully equipped with greener grass and taller trees. Rodney Train appeared clumsily, simply dropped from the sky since Taftly wanted to rush straight to the beating he was to give Train. Here the details were more successful. Train's right index finger had a tan-line band where the mood ring had been. His hair was unkempt and cackling, a nice effect which made Taftly smile. To heighten the tension, Taftly allowed Train two sucker punches. The last drew blood, at which point Taftly wiped his lip clean and proceeded to work Train over with kicks and chops so quick and forceful the air grew smokey. When Train hit the ground, his teeth were sundered, his brain spectacularly addled, and his hair had gone flat.

Taftly's eyes watered in both worlds as he turned to Fay. There she was, but there, too, was Dennis Jolly. Taftly concentrated and attempted to brush Dennis away. He rearranged the front porch, softened the streetlight, added a hanging fern, but Dennis resisted revision. "Oh, fuck you, Dennis Jolly and the space contraption you rode in on," Taftly said, then cranked and drove to the Starvin Marvin.

Dennis meanwhile had gotten himself into trouble. He'd called the state penitentiary but had been greeted with a recording. This annoyed him so he called back and left a bomb threat. Doing this, Dennis was sure, confirmed his genius. What, after all, would happen when a prison received a bomb threat? Where would they put all the convicts? It would be a mess. They might break out in all the commotion. Of course, maybe they'd just let the inmates stay put. They were criminals, after all. Why hadn't anyone thought of this before? Dennis had to hand it to himself. He was doing just this when Sheriff Williams phoned him.

"Dennis, this is Sheriff Williams."

"Howdy, Sheriff."

"Right. Listen. Did you call the state pen tonight?"

"Yep. And they slackin. Nobody answered the telephone. So I left them a little wake-up call."

"Yep, I know. And if it wadn't for me, you'd be gettin a little wake-up call yourself. If it wadn't for me, you'd be going to the pen yourself, come to think of it."

"What for?"

"You made a bomb threat you idiot. That's a felony."

"It was a joke. They ought to answer the damned phones and they wouldn't get threats. What if one a them prisoner's mamas was dying and couldn't get through? What if there was a pardon on the line?"

"I don't know why they didn't pick up when you called Dennis, and I don't really care. You've ticked me off, though, because I've got to come out there and arrest you now."

Dennis went blank.

"Dennis?"

He went a little blanker.

"It's Taftly's fault. He made me do it."

"Tell Taftly Rodney Train is still incarcerated. Then I want you to get your ass into town tomorrow first thing. If you're here by nine in the morning, I may not arrest you. If I have to come get you—"

"But sheriff, I got a big project going—"

"Nine o'clock." The sheriff hung the phone up. There was no law in the land worth having to spend several hours with Dennis Jolly. He'd give him a talking-to in the morning then send him on his way.

Taftly cut off his lights and waved to Brian.

"Mind if I steady myself in here for a bit?" he asked as he walked in the door.

"No, man. Totally cool."

"The steadying involves whisky." Taftly peeked a pint of bourbon from the pocket of his granddaddy's Barbour. "That all right?"

"Awesome," Brian enthused, proud to be taking part in some form of manly delinquency. "I'll keep a look out for the law."

"Thanks," Taftly said, walking to a booth at the back of the store.

Brian was explaining that he'd just highlighted his hair back to its original color while he fetched Taftly a chicken-on-a-stick. Taftly tried to wave it off, but once deposited in front of him he began devouring it. "What do you mean your original color?"

"These lighter ones are my original color. I had to bring a picture of me in to get it right."

"So it's colored to look like your hair would have looked if you'd just left it alone."

"Yep. Pretty cool, huh?"

"Pretty cool," Taftly agreed.

He was thinking of asking for another chicken-on-a-stick when the front door swung wide. Taftly looked over to see who it was and blanched. He blanched so thoroughly he thought of the word itself.

"Hey, Doctor Stevens."

"Howdy, Brian."

The doctor stood flat-footed, rubbing his head. Taftly recalled the bachelor party at the tavern years ago. The fellow standing before him had aged quite a bit, Taftly observed with satisfaction. He was wearing the kind of crisp jeans that doctors always wear, jeans that were not only clean but had never been dirty. He wore a pressed flannel shirt and a corduroy jacket, something Taftly grudgingly acknowledged as a tasteful touch. Even from a distance Taftly could see the untroubled surgeon's hands and fingers, the slick supple wrists, the boyish forearms. But what struck Taftly as incongruous were his eyes. They weren't the confidant and condescending kind doctors usually peer out from. They were, in fact, wincing, unsure and perhaps even tortured. Though Taftly could hardly believe it, he thought he detected fear in them.

"You're up late," Brian was saying.

"Yeah, I know. Way past my bedtime. I'm not feeling too well though. Can't sleep, either, and I didn't want to disturb Fay."

Brain smiled shyly. "Man, she's...." He blushed and ducked his head. "She's beautiful."

The doctor chuckled kindly and rocked back onto his heels. "Thank you, Brian. I think so, too," he said.

"So d'ya run outta aspirin?"

"No. No headache tonight. I'm probably just restless more than anything."

As the doctor walked over to the cooler, he caught Taftly staring at him. He nodded politely. Taftly noted the humility of this gesture, the easy-going kindness. He reached into his coat pocket to freshen his drink.

"I'd kill for one of those," the doctor said.

"You're welcome to one," Taftly said cheerfully. His voice was so poised and ready he did not recognize it. "Have a seat," he went on, offering the other side of the booth with authority. Taftly realized then that the voice belonged to his granddaddy, whose unfailing aplomb was never more impressive than during a crisis.

"Well, if you don't mind." The doctor poured himself a diet coke, Taftly noticed, then took a seat. "I haven't had a game drink since college. Thanks."

Taftly placed the Early Times before the doctor. "A sure

cure I've found," he said. "For most anything."

Taftly was glad to have his granddaddy along with him. Together they would do nicely. Once the doctor had become tight enough, Taftly believed there would be ample opportunity to learn a few things.

The doctor stirred and sipped and his pained eyes twinkled. He ran his fingers through his sandy hair. His hairline was receding, marking a pasty-white parabola. A some-time phrenologist, Taftly studied the doctor's head more closely. It was almost a miniature head though not freakish. There were no structural signs of dementia or blatant stupidity. Taftly did not believe the shape of it to be significant.

"Hits the spot. You from around here?"

"No. I live over in Copiah Springs."

"Mm-huh. Nice little town."

The doctor paused, telling himself to slow the interrogation. He'd already spotted the Fury in the parking lot and was anxious to learn more about his new stranger friend who was possibly a creep. Given Taftly's identical agenda, they were both behaving with courteous and cautious hesitation, like polished spies feeling about with kid-gloves, careful of fingerprints and yet determined to gain a firm grasp.

"So what brings you our way?"

"I like to get out and roam around sometimes. It's in my blood, I guess."

As soon as Taftly said this a swale of panic tipped him, but not over. He fortified himself with a long pull and remained quiet, thinking of his father.

"I don't get to roam around much anymore," the doctor stated. "Course, I don't much want to. I'd be happy to live out the rest of my days just like they are now."

Taftly believed the doctor was splendid and worthy just for saying such a thing. Here was a man who valued Fay and knew how to appreciate her. Deep in his heart it made him happy and therefore sad, sad because if he felt this way it meant he truly loved her, Fay, with an abiding love, one that was selfless and would not go away even though she belonged to the good doctor.

With his jeweled teeth and nails, his tidy mode of dress, his scrubbed refinement, none of which could hide his most redeeming feature, that he was in agony, perhaps this Stevens, M.D. deserved Fay. Taftly did not know for what reason, but the doctor was clearly distinguished by travail. Why, God might have a Total View, after all, Taftly thought. He felt like offering praise for the fact that Fay had been taken away from him and put in such deserving hands. He might have clapped had he not recognized his thoughts were at least as much the product of self-contempt as they were of admiration for a successful rival.

"That your Fury?" the doctor questioned, startling Taftly. He was almost certain Taftly wasn't a creep. Maybe he was just a special case of something. Nevertheless, the doctor needed more information.

"Sure."

"You don't see many of those anymore."

"It was my mother's."

"Does your mother live in Copiah Springs?"

"She did. She passed away."

"I'm sorry."

Taftly suddenly felt lost, forgotten, even by himself, so he said: "She had a hard life. I wish I could have made it better. That's one thing I wish I could do over."

At first it seemed the doctor had not even been listening. Taftly looked up to find his throat bobbing. He'd tilted back into a greedy drinking posture and when finished glared at Taftly with something approaching anger. "You never know about things sometimes. How they'll go. It burns me."

"That's the truth," Taftly offered.

"My wife comes from the perfect family. I joined her father's practice. Great fella. Her older brother was some kind of miracle athlete. All-state in high school football. Straight As. And boy, were he and Fay close. They were only two years apart and he was her life, really. I mean, if you knew her, clearly, she's a daddy's girl, but she also belongs to John, her brother. And he took care of her, too. God help you if you messed with her because he would be on you—*seriously* on you." The doctor shook his head slowly and sought another long swig. "And she was all about him, let me assure you," he said, before taking it.

Taftly was wondering why this brother hadn't ever decimated Train long ago when the doctor began again.

"Spring of his senior year—he's not drinking, not partying, not nothing—he's just driving right out on this highway here and it was raining and he hit some water and hydroplaned his way into paralysis. Hit a tree. God amighty. That was it. Took his legs from him. Could of taken his life. He was lucky. That's the kind of shit we doctors say when it's like that. 'He's lucky, considering.' Right. But damnit if he didn't fight back. I wouldn't have, I can tell you. I would have wheeled my ass right out a window." The doctor made a vigorous motion with his arms as if he were pushing a wheel chair. "But he fought like hell."

The doctor looked Taftly over and then looked past him. Taftly poured into both cups and waited. He knew very little about Fay he now realized. He felt a whole new love growing for her, for all the parts of her he'd never have the chance to become acquainted with.

"He was a terrific hunter and so they bought him a hydraulic deer stand. Can you imagine. I've seen it. Zoop! Up it goes. He did all the wheelchair sports. And then something truly amazing happened. After his first year of college, he starts dating this girl and they end up pregnant and married." The doctor was nodding vigorously. "Unreal. I said he was a fighter. And he was."

Taftly wondered if Fay had ever told the brother about him. He hoped so. He wanted the brother to think highly of him and maybe even to secretly wish that his baby sis' had married Taftly Harper.

"And then the kicker," the doctor said, setting his cup down. "He's driving down the road with a friend and they crash. Crash. *Fucking crash.* The friend was trying to put ketchup on his french fries and before he knew it they were flying off the road into an oak tree. And that was that. That was John. Two critical accidents in one lifetime. What are the odds of that? Huh? Just tell me, cause I'd like to know." He slammed his fist into the table.

"Fay was supposed to go to Vanderbilt like her daddy but she went over to Copiah College because, because, I guess, she couldn't go away after that. She was never really the same. So I've been told. She's perfect in my book, but I've heard that it took a lot out of her. She loved him more than...what am I saying? She *loved* him. Nothing more need be said. And when you love someone like that it's impossible to conceive of life without them. But then you go on living. What choice is there? That's what I'd like to know."

Taftly looked straight into the cork ceiling, into the tiny holes and vectors so much like a night sky. He held there, trying to keep the tears down.

"And you know what? You really know what? You think it's not worth it until one day it looks like it might be over and then, shit, then, of all times, you wish more than anything in the world that you had more—more life, the life you hated, any kind of life." The doctor placed his hands around his cup. His fingers touched it gently, reverently, as if preparing to exalt some holy chalice. "Sometimes I just don't know," he said quietly. "All I wanted was to take care of her. To make things right. To be there for her. That's *my* life." The doctor looked angry again. "Shit," he said.

"But you are taking care of her," Taftly protested.

The doctor sucked air and clicked twice. When he brought his head up, he was changed, controlled. He smiled and held out his hand. "I'm Tom Stevens by the way."

"Taftly," Taftly told him. "Taftly Harper."

This brought the doctor's eyes up in a flash of strained wonder. "Harper? Taftly Harper?" The doctor was unable to hide his concern about this. "So you're a Harper, huh?"

"I'm afraid I'm the end of the line," Taftly said. He could feel his granddaddy skeedaddling away with a growl, leaving him to fend off the doctor's interest alone.

"That's quite a family," the doctor was saying to himself. He began studying Taftly with clinical precision, something that made Taftly's hair quilt. "I believe that...matter of fact...." He snapped his fingers and then stopped and looked out the window. "Taftly Harper," he whispered.

"Taftly Harper," Taftly said nervously. He wanted to watch the doctor, to learn what was going on, but he was afraid and decided to wait out his fate.

"My wife has spoken of you," the doctor said finally.

"Fay?"

"Yes. Fay."

The doctor screwed his mouth into a pout, but carefully. He glanced toward the Fury then back to Taftly, looking him over bluntly. An unwanted nudeness come over Taftly then, as if his skin were performing lewd and shameless tricks. His ears felt as swollen and blood-rich as two tweaked nipples. His lips were in motion and appeared to be chanting to his lap. It seemed as if a rude hand were presently to shove his face into his ruined loins, doubling him over and breaking his back into a position of compromise.

"She's spoken very highly of you, as a matter of fact." The doctor paused. He paused again. "She's fond of you," he said. "I suppose I owe you a word or two of thanks actually. What you did to that asshole. God bless you."

Taftly could not believe it had come to this. He had braced for retribution, not redemption, and hardly knew how to handle the doctor's appreciation. "He had it coming," Taftly whispered.

"Yes, you're right. The bastard deserved it. But not everyone gets what's coming to them. And they should." The doctor was grim once more and Taftly again wondered what he had in mind regarding Taftly. "A Fury," he said, nodding, satisfied.

Their eyes joined in some shared pain though only the doctor knew the outcome, the prognosis. He wanted to tell Taftly everything, but after a moment it felt as if his mouth had been sprung loose from the need to speak by a small happy rainbow. He stood. "I'd better get back home," he said.

Taftly nodded and took his hand. "It was good to meet you."

The doctor waved to Brian and headed toward the door.

Halfway, he turned around. "You remind her of her brother, by the way," he said.

"I what?"

"Her brother. Something about you."

"She said that?"

"No. But now I know. I've figured it out. It was good to meet you, Taftly Harper. Good luck."

XVIII

Dear Taftly,

It was a pleasure getting to know you the other night. Fay's taste is impeccable, and I suppose that's been proven once again. I needed and enjoyed the talk, not to mention the bourbon. For most of my life, I've been pretty tight-lipped, but lately that's changed, and I find I want to tell people what's on my mind and right away. So I thought to drop you this note to say so.

Yours faithfully,
Thomas Stevens

PART
3

XIX

DENNIS HAD ADVICE. HAD IT CONSTANTLY.

"Don't ever be one of them stoics," he warned after finding Taftly napping in his rocking chair. A colossal harvest moon had arrived on the other side of the pond and for a sleepy moment Taftly thought Dennis had just descended from its peachy surface. Dennis walked over jauntily, provoked and provocative, a rankled candidate freshly ejected from a teeming twilight world that would not have him. All around the sky exhaled a sweet nacreous light, but Dennis was stubbornly resistent to such resplendent graces.

As if in defiance, he cleared his throat harshly. Something caught and Dennis placed his hands upon his knees, the better to be rid of the offending item. Though the blockage proved to be a rather trivial helping of phlegm, Dennis's heaving and wretching became so intense Taftly believed he was witnessing some devilish child-birth.

And then Dennis was upon the very porch, talking. "I'm serious. The holidays have made this clear to me."

"What are you talking about?"

"Stoics. Don't be one."

Dennis said this as if Taftly were presently to leap from a mountain top and plummet to his death. The urgency made Taftly's three fillings tune up like struck gongs.

"Don't, don't, don't. Just don't," Dennis was saying.

"Why not?"

"'Cause it's chicken shit is why not."

"Being stoic is being chicken shit?"

"You got it."

"No, I don't."

"There's a lot of talk in circles about stoics. Man wrote a novel praising 'em. But be warned. Stoic ain't nothing but a sheep in wolf's clothing. Hell, anybody can just take whatever comes their way. It's better than being a crybaby maybe but it ain't living. Anybody can just accept things. Just keep their mouth shut. Well, scratch that last." Dennis scratched his head then. Next he scratched his arm, carefully avoiding his pet scabs. "Shit," he said, renewed. "Stoic ain't Christian, neither. You member what that ole Arcus Aurilious did, don't ya?"

Taftly was dumbfounded and shook his head like a mule trying to throw a harness. "*Arcus?*"

"Arcus. Arcus Aurilious."

"I see."

"Well, he was a stoic. Hated Christians. So he burned 'em and fed 'em to the lions. And ya know what?"

"What?"

"They would cry out and sing their glories to God while being persecuted. And *then* guess what?"

"Mm-huh."

"It made ole Arcus mad cause them people were alive and for good reason, but he was just a yes man to fate. And ya know what happened to Rome after that on account a that fiddle and all."

"Sure," Taftly said.

"'Nother thing. Few years back a man was mass murdering people left, right and center if you please. Like to've never caught him. Know how they did?"

Taftly did not want to—

"Sombitch walked into a store an' the owner takes a look at this leather jacket he's awearing and couldn't believe it. Hadn't never seen one like it. Know why? I'll tell ya. Wadn't no seams to it. Seamless. Not a stitch on the damned thing. Guess how come? Cause it was made of gen-u-wine human flesh, that's how come. He'd found him some ole boy that fit him to a T and cut a coat out of him. Ain't that something? Now I asked ya—how in the living hell do you be a stoic when a man's walking around in broad daylight wearing a seamless human coat?"

Taftly had no answer but the macabre murder story was the last thing in the world he wanted to hear. Lately he'd begun to suspect he was being followed. Though he reminded himself Train was still incarcerated, he couldn't shake the sense that someone was tailing him. One night, in fact, he'd been almost positive a figure wearing a dark ski-mask had tip-toed behind him as he walked a back street just off the square. Why did Dennis always have to generate such stinging chaos?

Eventually these engagements began to drive Taftly back into town. He needed whisky and needed to be drinking it far from Dennis. Taftly was perpetually numb because of the new Dennis. And Dennis, for his part, was perpetually harping on Taftly for sleeping too much. Taftly believed Dennis to be a horrific dumbed-down Thomas Edison, pestiferous and always awake. It made Taftly wish he'd been more careful about what he'd wished for, for Taftly had wished that Dennis wasn't such a chattery lounger and now it was clear there were worse things that Dennis could be, chattery and industrious, for instance.

Taftly also suspected Dennis was interrupting something important, like his life. Taftly's visit with the doctor had left him cloudy on all fronts, uncertain of how he felt or how he should feel, but he had begun to believe something momentous might occur if he could just get Dennis to stop talking. Yet the closer it got to what Dennis kept calling the Big Birthday, the more like a noisome pestilence sent directly from God Dennis seemed.

Two weeks out from Christmas Dennis came at Taftly with a beef against materialism so extreme Taftly thought of pulling a Van Gogh on his ears. Dennis kept saying he had the cure: "Got the cure! Everbody'll know soon enough! You an' me, Taft! We gone set 'em back fer awhile, give 'em something ta think on!"

Taftly wanted to tell Dennis that he was not involved in his battles against materialism, nor any other "ism" or "ology," but the point seemed pointedly pointless, and so instead he fled his property.

When he walked into the Copiah Harper Tavern, he found Oswald guffawing fiendishly.

"You something," he said, jabbing a dirty finger in Taftly's direction. "I buy the tortured part."

Taftly clinched his fists. He had no idea what Oswald was talking about, but recognized in him someone who was smaller than himself and therefore a perfect first victim. He was moving in when Charlie hailed him. "You'd better come here," he said.

"What is it?"

"It's bad, brother. Somebody put these damned things up all over town." He handed Taftly a flyer. "I took all the ones down that were around the square, but Oswald was spying on the sorority girls and claims they're all over campus."

Taftly beheld the flyer.

TORTURED GENIUS TAPED LIVE!
UNEDITED LECTURES FROM TAFTLY HARPER ON GOD AND MANY OTHER GREAT THINKERS!

YOU WILL NOT BELIEVE YOUR EYES!
ONE DAY THESE TAPES WILL BE WORTH MILLIONS BUT YOU
CAN HAVE THEM FOR JUST $9.95!
WARNING: NOT FOR MINORS!
(THESE TOP-QUALITY CASSETTE TAPES ARE THE PRODUCT
OF A GENUINE TORTURED GENIUS WHO USES FOUL
LANGUAGE—MUST BE 18 TO ORDER. OR OLDER.)
CALL 876-3929
DENNIS JOLLY, INC.

Taftly felt the kind of dry sickness men complain of after having been gut shot, which reminded him: "I'm gonna kill Dennis."

"Better get them flyers down first," Charlie advised.

So many memories were crowded with flyers—dormitories where Taftly had once fumbled after dates, the library where he'd studied them, the cafeteria, the campus post office, even the austere lyceum with its heavy-footed columns that appeared diaphanous by the cold light of a sweetheart winter moon. All of these places held rich remembrances for Taftly and now handbills alleging his deranged brilliance.

Once the laziest occupant of the planet, Dennis had managed to cover every available space. Trees, cracks, crevices, byways and horribly even bathroom walls had been plastered with the testimonials. There were two colors, pink and pinker. The outrage! Taftly reeled about campus like a man beset with an affliction too grotesque to name, buzzing profanely as he snatched up the pink and pinker advertisements.

At the student union he nearly faltered. There were several large bulletin boards where students posted communiques of every sort and hundreds of these had been taken down and crammed into a trash bin. In place of which rested Dennis's handiwork, the walls from floor to ceiling pink and pinker.

Already there was a crowd. Dozens of students and shabby fellow travelers gathered to read the pronouncements, plucking them from the walls with ugly vigor. Peals of wicked laughter bloomed petals as sinister as Baudelaire's flowers. Taftly heard Dennis's name called and then his own. He even thought he heard gunfire and began to pipe out his breathing in pained whistles that sounded like the carping of a kettle. "Stop!" he shouted. But he quickly realized he had not shouted at all. In fact, he had not even opened his mouth.

He pushed to the boards, trembling, his horrible teeth clicking and chattering. He swiped to clear his name. He swiped again when a girl with dark curls and wild blue eyes began reading aloud just behind him. Her voice was sporting and cheerful and Taftly intended to strangle her, kinking her neck like a hose to stop the flow.

But when he turned to face her, she halted his progress completely. The girl was ridiculously beautiful, filled with such energy that Taftly felt a few years dead by comparison. And she was reading about him, about Taftly, by way of Dennis Jolly. It was a calamity beyond reckoning.

"Can you even believe this?" she drawled. "I can't wait to call the number."

"Let me see that." Taftly snatched the flyer.

The girl snatched it back. "Hey, buster. That's mine." She made a toy fist and shook it.

Taftly stared full on and was inflamed. "These are deeply wrong," he managed. He nodded, intending to convey earnestness, but feared his dimples were combusting.

He turned away and began tearing at the remaining flyers, yet within seconds the girl was at his back, shooting kitten hands between his waist and elbow, flushing him to the bone with fissures of delight while laying claim to the promise of lectures concerning God and other great thinkers.

"Just tell me why you're taking them down?"

"Because they're a violation."

She snapped her fingers. "Oh, that's right. They're a violation." She tapped her toe. "Of what exactly?"

The girl looked at Taftly without a hint of condescension or disregard. In fact, she seemed to somehow be on Taftly's team, though she'd obviously switched tactics, spoofing the disaster instead of trying to undo it. She wore a dapper pea coat and pearls. Little bracelets with school girl charms jangled about her wrists, making friendly tinkling noises. Her happiness made a place for Taftly and Taftly wanted to walk to that place.

"Who are you anyhow?" she asked.

"Tom Stevens." Taftly winced. Using the doctor's name smacked of some squalid blasphemy. Taftly wanted to add a truth to his duplicity to even it out, but squeels and titters erupted a few feet away as a glittery collection of coeds closed in on the bulletin board. "This is a violation!" he barked.

"Like we're going to get arrested," one of the girls remarked.

Taftly missed the comment. His outburst had reminded him of something he was sure was important, something he'd heard somewhere before that was connected to the regrettable scene before him. He thought of a night highway. He thought of aliens. He thought of Dennis. As students brushed past him to get at him he thought of the things he'd shouted beneath the moonlight by the pond and shook his head. The truth of Taftly Harper was out at last.

This should have been the worst thing that had ever happened to him, bad enough to allow him the privilege of considering himself a loser again. By rights, there was every chance of his regaining access to a life of guiltless depression. Yet with each flyer a passerby peeled from the walls, Taftly was beginning to feel as if something unwanted were being peeled from his dizzy heart. It felt lighter. The more he thought of it, there was something strangely liberating about the way he'd been smeared across town, the way people were taking him home for laughs and the way it seemed not to matter. He hadn't spoken to more than ten or so people in better than a year and now his name was on everyone's lips and everyone was happy and why not? *Taftly, by god, you're right in the thick of things,* Taftly thought. He believed he would break down and laugh.

"Know what I think?" It was the girl. "I think *you're* Taftly Harper." She nudged the tip of Taftly's desert boot, fixed him with a tender pout, then shrugged and began taking flyers down.

"Never mind that," Taftly said.

"Never mind what?"

"The flyers. Never mind them. It doesn't matter."

Taftly thought about this. When he looked up he found the girl was still there, waiting. "My name's Darl, as in Darling, not Darla," she said.

Taftly stuck his hand out. "Taftly Harper." He smiled. It seemed obvious what he should do and already he knew her answer.

When they entered the Copiah Harper Tavern the reliables began sniggering and sending up waves of mock applause. Taftly bowed graciously and ordered two beers. Charlie looked Taftly's guest over approvingly. "Taft," he said, grinning.

Taftly removed a flyer from Oswald's hand. It was pinker. He grinned and handed it back. The flyers pleased him now. He was still going to do something terrible to Dennis, but there was ample time for that. Besides, having a drink with this girl seemed to be the necessary preliminary event for any future course of action. Why hadn't he thought of this sooner? What could have possibly possessed him to remove himself from such mercy, such time-honored, God-given comfort? He thought of the Clydesdales, as an answer, and then of Fay, as another, but those tragic tidings seemed to not be enough of a reason anymore. *Just what the hell have you been doing with yourself, Taft,* Taftly demanded.

Darl sat very close after a second round. Taftly had not developed a plan for such good luck and it showed. Everything she told him was exactly right in the way that nitrous oxide is exactly right. He'd known her for fifteen minutes and was already drafting behind her bold embrace of each moment, the main trick to passing time profitably, the trick that old dogs vaguely remember as something once dreamt and never lived.

"So what are you doing over the holidays besides being recorded?" Darl asked.

"Going on a killing spree."

"Oh, great. How many people are involved?"

"Just one. But I'm going to kill him over and over again."

Darl caught and held Taftly solid with her eyes, kissing his knuckles with her own. "Well, Merry Christmas, Taftly Harper," she said.

XX

TAFTLY WALKED FROM HIS HOUSE toting an axe. On his way to the deluxe shack he nearly spooked the life out of two college boys treading up the footpath with a small box of tormented genius tapes. Taftly told the one carrying the box to drop it. Whatever the young man had learned in school, he knew at least this much—he needed to put the box on the ground immediately and back away.

"If you gentlemen will excuse me, I'm on a bit of a rampage now," Taftly explained. At that he struck home, shattering the plastic cassettes. The box held to the axe, affording Taftly the opportunity to chop it into the ground for awhile. After having destroyed it to his satisfaction, he noticed the young men were gone. It was time to see about Dennis.

Dennis had just then come out to investigate the racket. Taftly was too far away for Dennis to discover exactly what he was doing, but from the look of things he figured Taftly might be planting something, maybe a secret manuscript. "Wish I could get this on film," he muttered. "Video footage'll definitely be my next project. That'd go like hot cakes."

Dennis took a seat in his chaise lounge chair with a book in his lap, speculating on his next enterprise. He'd made a few purchases recently: wire-rim spectacles, a tweed blazer, a pair of scrubs, a pipe, a giant tin of cherry tobacco and a new cap, worn like the old one. So equipped, he looked like a prop in a haunted house designed by a kindergarten of deviant underachievers, though he felt himself to be costumed along the lines of an eccentric entrepreneur.

"Howdy, partner," he said when Taftly walked over. "You ain't gonna believe what all I've done."

Taftly smiled a very rough smile. "You were right about the stoics," he said evenly.

"Huh?"

"The stoics."

"Oh, yeah. But that ain't all." Dennis stopped. He'd spotted the axe. "Hey, what ya doing with that axe?"

Taftly brought the axe head to rest on the porch with a dull thud, then placed both hands atop the handle and leaned forward. "A man shouldn't just accept things."

"Hell no. Matter a fact—"

Taftly interrupted him sharply. "Know what's keeping you alive Dennis?"

"You drunk?"

"Why, yes, I am. Know what's keeping you alive?"

"Keeping me alive?"

"That's right. You curious?"

Dennis had edged from concern to outright fear. "I'm curious 'bout a lot of things. Like that there axe."

Taftly leaned forward and whispered the answer into Dennis's ear. Dennis jumped back, scandalized. "Shit. Ain't had none in years," he protested.

"Never mind that."

Dennis sprang from the porch as soon as Taftly gained it. He said not a word when Taftly chopped through his locked front door and kicked it down. He moaned a little when he heard Taftly laying into the high-speed duplicator and a little more when Taftly called out that he'd found the box marked originals. A burgundy ski-mask flew into the yard through the hole where the front door had been. After that Dennis heard what sounded like a brawl, grunts and screams, things breaking apart, objects thrown, plastic crushed and crushed again, and toward the end a maniacal laughter which continued until Taftly was standing in the door way, the axe shouldered, holding a Christmas ball in his hand which he crushed and dusted the porch with.

An unwanted looseness came over Dennis's bowels then. He was convinced the silence would drive Taftly to decapitate him. What with his new cap and all, it seemed a shame.

"Them tapes was the most hairbrained idea—"

"Don't remind Taftly of the tapes," Taftly said.

"Don't remind Taftly of the tapes. Got it. Say, what's in yer pocket."

"Oh, these?" Taftly held up some forty pages titled *The Life and Times of Taftly Harper* by D. Ernest Jolly. "They look interesting."

"Hey, hold on now. That's mine. That's my personal private property." Though still frightened, Dennis was truly outraged. "Them tapes is straight up you, fine, but that there is part mine. I aimed to finish it and combine...."

Taftly was close to him now. "I'll give it a read. Tell you what I think."

"But you can't! That's mine! I ain't finished with it yet!"

"You're finished, Dennis. Merry Christmas. We're having Christmas together, by the way. Me, you and Pastor Bates." Taftly dug in his pocket and pitched Dennis a set of keys. "You can have your present early. They're to the rice burner. It runs fine. You're going to need to get into town for a new door and I don't want to be seen with you."

"Course not," Dennis stated emphatically. "Who would? Most of the time I don't even want to be seen with me."

After Taftly had gone into the house, Dennis remained in the yard. He didn't feel too badly but still he felt like crying.

XXI

TAFTLY BOUGHT A CHRISTMAS TREE and even decorations and twinkling lights. He spruced up his house and began cooking. By Christmas Eve he'd exhausted himself and realized that he'd gone twenty-four-hours without a cocktail.

In addition to a shapely ten-foot scotch pine, he'd purchased a miniature singing Christmas tree which he placed on an end table in his living room. It wore a Santa cap and had a motion sensor for a nose. Each time something crossed it, the tree erupted into a chorus of jingle bells, its swollen plastic eyes glowing an unseemly preternatural green as it flapped its branches. The thing was nothing short of terrifying. Taftly kept forgetting it existed and had several times set it off and been reminded of its creepy crooning presence so forcefully he spilled his drink. He would have put the tree away but was hoping it might do something funny to Dennis.

Taftly was reading his life and times when Pastor Bates arrived. "I've got some Christmas ingredients," Pastor Bates told him. "Milk punch. I allow myself a little of that every year. Hey, what ya got there?"

"Oh, nothing. Just some old papers."

They walked into the kitchen. Pastor Bates found a punch bowl and filled it with several gallons of whole milk. He added vanilla and confectionery sugar. "Nutmeg," he said. "I forgot nutmeg. You got any?"

Taftly found it and watched Pastor Bates stir.

"Like mine with nutmeg," Pastor Bates informed him. He unscrewed the cap to a fifth of Old Charter and emptied it into the bowl.

"Like yours with bourbon, too."

"Just a little. Where's Mr. Jolly? Wouldn't be Christmas without him."

"Don't worry. He'll be here soon enough."

Pastor Bates chuckled. "He used to come to church every Sunday. We'd have someone come out here to pick him up. But then he insisted that we give him a Sunday School class cause he wanted to teach. I told him we'd think about it and that didn't suit him at all. Became very critical of my sermons. That's when I discovered he's not an idiot."

"No, he can surprise you." Taftly accepted a mug of punch and led the way into the living room. He opened the drawer to the end table and placed the pages inside. Reading them had been a thrilling if deeply nauseating experience, something like riding a roller-coaster while suffering from a case of double-pneumonia. Dennis wasn't a terrible writer, it turned out, though imagining the pages being read by anyone else made Taftly grow a second-skin of cold sweat.

It would be a mistake to think of Mr. Taftly Harper merely as a deeply depressed wise man, for he is more, much more, than that. He is very fashionable, for instance. My careful research indicates he didn't have fancy clothes when he was growing up. Well, it should surprise no one that he has more than made up for those lost years. . . .

"So he wanted a Sunday School class, huh?"

Oh, yeah. Did he ever. Nobody else was teaching the Bible right or something. And a few months after he left the church he accosted me—and that's the right word, too, *accosted*—right there on the square. He went into this long and very loud speech about how he forgave me for the error of my ways."

Taftly was shaking his head.

"Anyhow," Pastor Bates continued, "That's just to say I wouldn't worry about that tape business."

Taftly wanted to ask Pastor Bates if he'd actually read one of the flyers but Dennis was upon them. He'd crept in like an unknown disease and they were defenseless against him. "Where's that axe?" he squalled. He fell on Pastor Bates with a hug. "Pastor, Merry Christmas. You lookin' at a man that near 'bout lost his life."

"How'd you nearly lose your life?"

"You ought to be askin' 'bout what saved it. You just wouldn't believe."

One interesting note, which I'll come back to in time, is that Taftly could do quite nicely with the ladies but doesn't. He seems to hide from them. From my extensive researches, I attribute this to excessive grieving over his mother or some other dark secret.

"Dennis," Taftly said.

Dennis tucked his thumbs into his belt and rocked back. It was at that moment that Taftly realized he was wearing an ankle-length camel's hair coat which he'd bought to compliment his new scrubs and combat boots. "How're the faithful?" Dennis was saying.

"Well and fine," Pastor Bates told him.

Dennis nodded tolerantly. "Been meaning to get back to church here lately. Mainly i been doing my own independent study. Book of Ezekial. Tell ya what. you crack that nut and you've accomplished something."

"It's a very difficult book," Pastor Bates acknowledged.

Taftly handed Dennis a drink. He drained it in three indecent gulps. "Hope there's not too much liqour in here. I'm not a drinker. You think I've got energy now, you ought to see me when I'm rolling."

"Be careful then. These are strong," Taftly warned.

I have come close to talking to Mr. Harper about his perpetual nipping many times but I have always stopped myself out of concern that it may be linked to his gifts.

"Hey. Maybe I'll have one more." Dennis fingered his nutmeg mustache but for some reason did not wipe it away. "Listen, Pastor. Let me know if ya wanna take a peek at my notes on Ezekial. I got pages."

"Here, let me take your coat," Taftly offered.

As Dennis began to unburden himself, his arm swung past the motion sensor of the miniature Christmas tree and it burst into song. Dennis shrieked and chopped it from the table. He sounded like a panther gone sissy.

"Dennis!" Taftly growled.

"What the hell was that?"

"A Christmas tree."

"You have any idea what a thing like that could do to children?" Dennis scolded.

"Do you see any children?"

"Not the point." Dennis placed his hand to his heart, feeling for irregularities. He was considering telling Pastor Bates what Taftly had done to his deluxe shack when he caught a whiff of something. "What's that smell?"

"Come on in," Taftly said. "It's ready."

Taftly had cooked a pork roast and a duck. He'd fixed rice and mashed potatoes and green beans and creamed corn. Pastor Bates had brought cornbread. Dennis had brought himself.

After the meal, Pastor Bates read the Christmas story. He said a prayer and they quickly began drinking again, growing chatty and merry, these three odd bachelors on Christmas Eve, one God's servant, one God's prodigal, one whose purpose was known to God alone.

"Speaking of which," Dennis announced. No one had said anything and his outburst startled them. "Y'all ever noticed all the weirdos occupying the planet?"

"I reckon I have," Pastor Bates said calmly.

"Yeah. Reckon you have," Dennis said and then said nothing more.

Neither Taftly nor Pastor Bates could abide the silence which followed. It was a Dennis silence, pregnant with absurdity. They knew it had to be stamped out, though not with more talk from Dennis.

"I think I'm going to get married," Pastor Bates announced. He had not wanted to say this, but once it came out he realized it was true.

Taftly looked over. "Seriously? Who are you seeing?"

"No one right now. But I believe it's going to happen. I think it's time."

"Wouldn't do it, Pastor," Dennis insisted.

"Huh?"

"No sir. Shore wouldn't."

"Wouldn't do what?"

"Marry is what."

"I think it's a great idea," Taftly stated.

"You ain't never been married neither. I speak with some limited authority pertaining here. And trust me with a capital T—don't do it."

"I'll take that under advisement, Dennis," Pastor Bates said.

"I ever tell you about Bunny, Pastor?"

Taftly said, "This is not the—"

Causing Dennis to become cross and parental. "Listen here. On this subject I'm the elder. Besides," he said, sweeping in their eyes, "if I know anything it's that I'm looking right at three fellers—"

"There's two of us aside from you," Pastor Bates corrected. He did so kindly but it won him great satisfaction.

"That's where yer plumb wrong, Pastor. 'Cause I got my eyes looking right back in my own head. Let him without sin, etcetera. And what I'm sayin' is we're three men who couldn't never be happy with no normal woman but what she had many a perversion. A long days ride from the high road, if you catch my drift. I'm lookin at three men destined to marry Bunnies."

Taftly was horrified. Pastor Bates was mystified. Both swifted down their drinks. Although believing himself to be something of a more dignified senior member, Dennis felt keenly a part of the club, and did likewise.

"Y'all want another?" Taftly called from the kitchen.

"Do birds fly into windows?" Dennis returned. "Does diarrhea run? Do bears—"

"That's enough, Dennis," Pastor Bates said in his best pastor's voice, shrinking an eye for emphasis.

Dennis was drunk and suspected the others were even more intoxicated and not bright enough for his word play. He would have to slow down for them.

"I heard you had a date the other night, Taftly." Pastor Bates rested his mug on his belly. His grin was fantastic. "Heard she was a pretty young lady."

"What young lady? I ain't seen hide nor hair of one," Dennis stated. It would not be good at all if something had happened that he didn't know about. He frowned.

"Hey, listen, Taftly. Good for you," Pastor Bates said.

Dennis grunted, exasperated. "How did it happen?"

"How did what happen?"

"This alleged date."

"She fell out of a space ship right into my lap," Taftly snapped. "How do you think it happened? I asked a girl out."

"You the grumpiest damned person I ever met in my whole life. I ever tell you that, Taft? Taft-*lee*. You probably done scared Santy Claus away."

Like most original thinkers, Taftly Harper is irritable almost all the time more often than not. It takes a great deal of work to be the neighbor of such a person because they are always grumbling and complaining. Some geniuses are blessed with good tempers and some are not. Taftly Harper's specialty is not being patient.

Dennis and Taftly stared at one another, their eyes locked with furious understanding.

"I can't tell you how many times I've had to play Santa Claus," Pastor Bates began. "Nobody ever brings me a pillow, neither. You'd think they'd bring me one just to keep from hurting my feelings."

Taftly clucked a heavy tongue and peered around the living room. He believed he'd done a credible job with it and hoped the others would notice. He'd even tinseled his favorite Elvis photograph, a grainy black and white of the King at a very young age, his arms around two girls with clever faces, his dark silk shirt knotted above his belly button. He was wearing eye-liner and looked out toward the camera with a piercing disregard Taftly admired to his marrow. It said: "Like I give a damn what the men think." Like I do, either, Taftly thought.

"So you're going to get married and ruin your life," Dennis said.

Pastor Bates had forgotten about his pronouncement. The circumstances which had fathered it were vague to him now and he felt embarrassed.

Dennis stood. "Don't say I never warned you."

"What do you need?" Taftly asked.

"I'll be back. Don't worry."

Taftly heard the front door slam and shrugged within his whisky slicker. Neither rain, nor sleet, nor snow could stop him now. Without realizing it, he was smiling.

"By the way, you seem almost happy."

Taftly looked over at Pastor Bates. "Happy?" He felt cheated of something. "I wouldn't say that."

"Just an observation. You seem different. But it's Christmas, after all."

"Yes. It's Christmas."

Pastor Bates's eyes were glassy. Though reclined, he felt as if he were leaning forward, the fire both drawing and holding him at the same time. In this teasing solid motion he thought he recognized the very form and habitat of contentment. But such sweetly insistent thoughts were interrupted by the sudden recollection of something Dennis had said.

"Hey, Taftly? What did he mean about us marrying bunnies?"

XXII

THEY WERE DRINKING HAPPILY when Taftly heard something. "You hear something?"

Pastor Bates looked over, tilting his head. "Yeah. It's coming from the roof."

Taftly listened. The tin was buckling loudly now, sending out shrill blankets of sound. Whatever it was had to be large, undoubtedly man-sized. Taftly instantly thought of Train—Train stalking him, Train coming down the chimney to butcher him for Christmas. The drunken concern on his face began to unnerve Pastor Bates.

"There it is again!" Taftly screeched.

They trained their ears hard to heaven and noted the ragged scampering above.

"Maybe its just a big old coon," Pastor Bates said.

"No, no. It's much bigger."

That was when they heard the first of the three "ho-ho-hos!" The Santa call was prodigious, the first "ho" notches above a scream. In the case of the second they detected fear, something gone direly wrong. The third was pathetic, a desperate careening howl that toward the end broke into an unmodulated and nervy wail. Stamping followed, then something crashed. Finally they heard a thud in the yard.

They found Clementine Jeffries standing over Santa Claus with his machette. "Shoulda knowed it was you!" Clementine cried.

Dennis lay flat of his back, tangled up in Christmas lights. The lights were still functioning and Dennis was blinking and moaning. He wore a velvet Santa suit. His Santa cap sat on top of his normal cap which was tight as a vice about his eyebrows. His new spectacles were bent. "Merry fucking Christmas," he said.

"Watch yo mouth round Pastor," Clementine told him.

"I ain't watching shit. I ain't figured out yet if I'm even alive."

"Are you all right?" Pastor Bates asked Dennis, dropping to his prayer knee.

"He come down pretty hard," Clementine allowed.

Dennis groaned. "I'd hate to die on Christmas an' ruin everbody's holiday," he lamented.

"Here. Let me help you up," Taftly offered. He was, for once, glad to see Dennis.

"I don't think I'd better. They may have ta bring a coptor in for me."

"Coptor my black ass," Clementine huffed. "Get up!"

"Sustainable trauma! Ever heard of it?" There were green and blue lights twinkling across Dennis's forehead and the bridge of his nose, but he knew he must bear up under this indignity just as any truly injured person would. "Plus I'm a fire hazard."

Clementine began clapping and doing a little dance. "Man, I wish y'all coulda *seen* it. I pulled up an' see somebody in a Santa suit creeping round up on da roof, banging an' making a racket. Den he starts "ho, ho, hoeing," an' gets caught all up in dem lights. Oh, man! He was stomping like they was snakes an' den he come right off the edge! All lit up! Oh, Taff!"

Dennis sat up. "Clem, lemme tell ya something," he said somberly. "I could last til next year and not miss you. And by next year I mean the year after the next year. Not just these next few days before the next next year."

Pastor Bates and Taftly took Dennis's hands. "Well, it was a good try," Pastor Bates said.

"Some people don't care, Pastor."

"I know it."

After de-lighting Dennis, they returned to the living room, where Dennis opened his sack of presents. He'd been crafting animal figures with sticks and twine. There were cows, pigs and dogs, according to Dennis, though only Dennis could tell the difference.

"Very clever, Dennis," Taftly told him.

"I'll put mine right on my desk," Pastor Bates said.

"It'll make ya think now," Dennis assured him.

Clementine looked at his and could conceive of nothing kind to say about it. As soon as he got a few miles down the highway he planned on throwing it out the window. "Come on out to the truck, Taffly. Wife made ya a fruit cake. Merry Christmas, y'all."

When Taftly returned with the fruit cake the living room was empty. He walked back to the guest bedroom and told Pastor Bates good night. Pastor Bates had to be up early to go to the hospital and then the nursing home and Taftly fetched him an alarm clock.

Taftly sliced a piece of cake and poured another mug of milk punch. He turned off the houselights to enjoy the fire and the Christmas tree. It was growing cold outside. The night was clear but a front was moving through and the town hoped for snow tomorrow. Taftly suddenly wondered where Dennis had gone. He decided he'd better check on him.

Dennis stood by the pond. He was wearing his camel hair coat again and stared across the water with great seriousness.

"You all right?"

Dennis didn't look over. "I'll make it," he said.

"What a night."

"Yeah. What a night. Better than last year though. Last year I spent Christmas by myself. Took a bus to see mama but it broke down. When the new one came, I don't know, I just didn't get on it. I just came back here."

"Where's your mama this year?"

"She's gone to have Christmas with some friends. She invited me and all, but said they really didn't have no room for me. I don't know. Maybe we'll get together after the New Year." Dennis removed a pack of Reds from his pocket and and shook one out. "Let's smoke one up for mama."

"Let's."

He handed Taftly a cigarrette. "I hate to be the clown so much. It gets old," Dennis said. He gave Taftly a light, then looked back over the water. "Seems like I always think I'm finally 'bout to accomplish something that'll make everbody proud, when it just turns out I've been Dennis again."

Taftly patted Dennis on the back. He realized it had probably been years since Dennis had actually touched another human being. It did not seem to be Dennis's fault anymore.

"I'm sorry about the tapes and the book and all. I really am. Cause you been a good friend to me, Taftly. Don't think I ain't noticed. You got your quirks but you're a fine young Christian man."

Taftly drew back. He couldn't stand to hear this. "Dennis," he said. He shook his head. "Think about all that stuff you taped. All the things I've said. Think about all the things I've done."

But Dennis wasn't listening. He was searching the sky for his chances. "Know what I wish," he said softly. "Wished I looked like you. First thing I'd do is get me a woman. It just gets lonely sometimes. But if I was handsome like you, Taft, hell, they might be a prayer in the world."

Taftly sat on his porch and waited for Christmas while stars fell like a gentle distant rain. He counted ten and let them be. He thought of Fay and the doctor. He thought of Dennis. It occurred to him then how much he wanted his life. It was like a secret present that had been kept in reserve for a special occasion and now, at last, had been opened. He was astounded to discover that he wanted more—more time, more life, the chance to feast on God's rich diet, millions and millions of Total Views. He knew he hadn't the stomach for it but hungered nonetheless. How strange that he had not wanted to go on when now it suddenly seemed clear that his only lasting regret would be that he could not go on and on. He thought of all the people who had been accompanying him these many months, the sufferers he forever fretted about, and realized his debt to them could only be paid by moving forward since he was able. He could hear them say they would if they had the chance and that they were and would he join them.

Epilogue

EARLY THE NEXT YEAR TAFTLY WAS SEEN walking the square with a man who looked like Taftly. This second Taftly was older and thinner, with fuller lips and eyes of cautious wonder. They sat together over coffee, talking hesitantly, but days later they were everywhere talking all the time.

Then the second Taftly left and Taftly made some changes. He gave his farm house and property to Dennis outright and moved into his granddaddy's fusty manse on the edge of town. He planted a vast garden and filled the old stables with several good riding horses. He hired Clementine to watch the stock market all day which he did between soap operas. He continued training with Dennis and paid for him to enroll in Copiah College, where Taftly had begun to teach literature. He bought a very fancy golden retriever.

Taftly whisked Darl about town for a year in a shiny new white Tahoe, then let her go to seek her place in the world. He wore coats and ties to class and dated coeds and was unwanted by some of the faculty. But the clause in the school charter was clear—any Harper descendant who wished to be president of the college could be so as long as the board approved it. A second proviso was that a majority of the board's members must come from town. And Copiah had longed to do Taftly a good turn for many years.

So when he reviewed these facts with the president, explaining that he did not wish to preside, but to teach, the president tenured him on the spot.

Every evening when Taftly walked into the tavern to claim his toddy, he'd finish his round of hellos, shake Charlie's hand, then look over his shoulder to the old photograph of his granddaddy with a sharp grin. *You old sombitch,* he thought. *You always knew what you were doing.*

During the spring of Taftly's thirty-fifth year Tom Stevens died. Cancer had taken his brain. It had been a long struggle. Tom Stevens had written Taftly an urgent letter on his death bed, but it had been sent to Taftly's old address where it fell into Dennis's hands and was lost. Taftly did not find out the doctor was dead until late that summer. He never learned of the letter.

But that was all right, for one afternoon that next fall Taftly was sitting behind his granddaddy's desk reading while a sweet chilly rain fell. He looked up from his book and saw a woman and a little girl advancing toward his front door, doctor's orders.

The great surprise of Taftly's life was that he was not surprised.